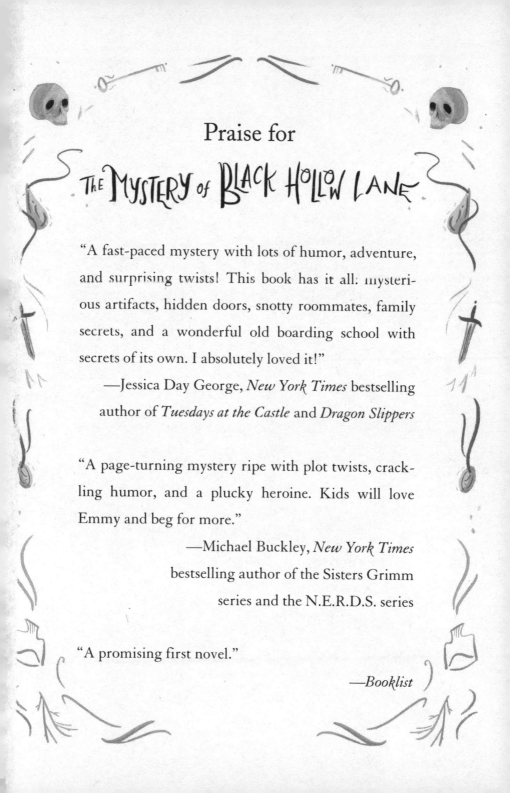

Praise for
The Mystery of Black Hollow Lane

"A fast-paced mystery with lots of humor, adventure, and surprising twists! This book has it all: mysterious artifacts, hidden doors, snotty roommates, family secrets, and a wonderful old boarding school with secrets of its own. I absolutely loved it!"

—Jessica Day George, *New York Times* bestselling author of *Tuesdays at the Castle* and *Dragon Slippers*

"A page-turning mystery ripe with plot twists, crackling humor, and a plucky heroine. Kids will love Emmy and beg for more."

—Michael Buckley, *New York Times* bestselling author of the Sisters Grimm series and the N.E.R.D.S. series

"A promising first novel."

—*Booklist*

The Mystery of Black Hollow Lane

The Mystery of Black Hollow Lane

Julia Nobel

sourcebooks
jabberwocky

TWEEN /

Published by Sourcebooks Jabberwocky, an imprint of Sourcebooks, Inc.
P.O. Box 4410, Naperville, Illinois 60567-4410
(630) 961-3900
Fax: (630) 961-2168
sourcebooks.com

Library of Congress Cataloging-in-Publication Data

Names: Nobel, Julia, author.
Title: The mystery of Black Hollow Lane / Julia Nobel.
Description: Naperville, Illinois : Sourcebooks Jabberwocky, [2019] |
Summary: Twelve-year-old Emmy investigates the connection between her father's
disappearance and a secret society at her prestigious English boarding school.
Identifiers: LCCN 2018010905 | (hardcover : alk. paper)
Subjects: | CYAC: Boarding schools--Fiction. | Schools--Fiction. |
Secret societies--Fiction. | Missing persons--Fiction. |
England--Fiction. | Mystery and detective stories.
Classification: LCC PZ7.1.N617 Mys 2019 | DDC [Fic]--dc23
LC record available at https://lccn.loc.gov/2018010905

Source of Production: LSC Communications, Harrisonburg, Virginia, United States
Date of Production: January 2019
Run Number: 5013964

Printed and bound in the United States of America.

LSC 10 9 8 7 6 5 4 3 2 1

To Ben, who loves to tell stories,
and to Linda, who loved to hear them.

CHAPTER 1

The Parenting Guru

There were certain things Emmy's mother didn't *really* need to know. Trivial things like whether Emmy had clipped her toenails or that she'd stepped in something sticky at the park. But the letter in Emmy's nightstand was not a trivial thing, and if her mom had found out about it, she would have pitched a fit. That's why Emmy was glad to be in New York City instead of at home in Connecticut. She wanted as much distance between her mom and that letter as possible, even if it meant suffering through another boring book launch.

"Having a good time, darling?" Emmy's mom said as she handed her a fancy-looking glass.

She took a sip and just about gagged. She didn't know what real champagne tasted like, but the fake stuff was like someone had dropped Pop Rocks into a bucket of rotting apples. She did her best to smile. Her mom was mad enough already.

"Thankfully, no one's noticed the bandage under your hat," her mom whispered. "Why you insisted on playing in that soccer game today is beyond me." She smiled and waved at one of the partygoers. "You knew my book launch was this evening, and yet…"

Emmy rubbed her forehead, where a ridiculous hat covered three fresh stitches. What was she supposed to say? *Sorry I'm a good soccer player, Mom. I'll try to suck more, that way I won't get on the good teams.* "I can't just skip a match, Mom. My team—"

"Your team can certainly do without you for one game, Emmeline."

Emmy cringed. It was never a good sign when her full name came out.

Her mom took a sip of champagne. "Listen Emmy, there's something we need to talk about after the party."

Emmy held her breath. Her mom didn't know about the letter, did she? If she'd found out...if she knew what Emmy was about to do...

"It's about my book tour."

Emmy breathed out and picked at the front of her dress. She had to put her search out of her mind tonight. The last thing she needed was her mom getting suspicious.

"After my tour is done, I have another project in the works. I don't want to get into the details now, but things will be a bit different. I just want you to be prepared."

The nerves wriggled back into Emmy's stomach. *Be prepared.* That's what her science teacher, Mrs. Henry, had said during their natural disaster drill last week.

"Pam, there you are!" A little blond woman bustled toward them, and Emmy tried not to groan. She usually avoided her mom's publicist at all costs.

Her mom kissed the woman's cheek. "Gretchen, you've really outdone yourself with this party."

"Anything for my number one client!" Gretchen turned to Emmy. "And don't you look lovely this evening! That hat is just perfect for you. It darkens your hair so that the red isn't nearly so shocking."

Gretchen smiled as if that were a compliment, but Emmy

knew better. She was used to people commenting on her orangey-red hair.

"I'm so glad you could be here tonight, it'll really play well with the crowd. Did you invite a few friends like I suggested?"

"Uh, nobody could make it." Emmy snatched a crab puff from a passing waiter's tray and stuffed it in her mouth. She hadn't invited anybody. She'd only been at her latest private school for a few weeks, and making friends had never been her strength. That would involve talking to people.

A man came into the restaurant lounge and Gretchen squealed. "Clint!" She grabbed him by the arm and practically shoved him at Emmy's mom.

"Pam, you remember Clint Markum from *Parenting Now* magazine?"

"Of course, Clint, nice to see you again."

"Hi, Pam, I just loved the new book!"

"Isn't it fabulous?" Gretchen said. "There's so much buzz right now. Everyone is calling her America's favorite parenting guru."

Emmy tried not to laugh. The only person she'd heard use that phrase was Gretchen, over and over, any time a reporter was in earshot.

"And this must be your daughter," Clint said. "It's Emmeline, right?"

Emmy blinked. "Oh, uh, yeah." She shuffled her feet. Reporters didn't usually talk to her, and that was the way she liked it.

"You must be very proud of your mom," Clint said.

Emmy nodded. Clint looked like he was waiting for her to say something else, but Emmy had no clue what it was.

"Raising you all on her own while managing a big career—it must be like having Superwoman at home!"

Emmy nodded again. Maybe if she didn't say anything, he'd stop asking her questions.

Clint cleared his throat and turned back to Emmy's mom. "Gretchen was telling me all about your new project. It sounds so exciting!"

Something flickered in her mom's eyes. No one else would have seen it—she was always composed in public—but to Emmy, that flicker revealed a tiny jolt of panic.

"I'm surprised Gretchen gave you a sneak peek," her mom said. "We were going to keep it under wraps for at least another week."

"I know," Gretchen said, "but this seemed like the perfect opportunity to strike while the iron is hot."

Emmy's mom smiled and nodded. "Emmy, why don't you get yourself something to eat?"

Emmy took a few steps toward the nearest waiter, but she didn't get very far.

"So, Pam, what made you decide to host a reality television show?"

Emmy whirled around. Her mom was going to be on TV? Her mom glanced at her. "It seemed like a wonderful opportunity to really engage with parents in a new way. We haven't finalized all the details yet, so I'd rather not say too much."

Clint looked at Gretchen. "What's the format like?"

"She's going to be fully immersed with families for a few weeks at a time," Gretchen said. "She'll tell them all the things they're doing wrong and whip them into shape."

"How exciting!" Clint said. "Is Emmeline going with you?"

Thump. Thump. Thump. Emmy's heart started beating a little harder. Her mom cleared her throat. "No, it'll be too chaotic."

"Who's looking after her?"

Thump. Thump. Thump.

Emmy's mom smiled widely, like a cheerleader who knows her team is about to lose. "I've found the most wonderful school. Emmy's going to love it. It will be like living with family."

Emmy wrinkled her pounding forehead. Schools weren't like families. It's not like she would be living at school... unless...her mom wasn't actually sending her to...

"A boarding school?" Clint finished Emmy's thought.

Thump-thump. Thump-thump.

"An all-inclusive immersion school," her mom said. "Emmy will be living with people her own age in a rich learning environment."

Emmy had no idea what an "all-inclusive immersion" school was, but it sure sounded like boarding school to her.

"Which school is it?" Clint asked. "Is it close by?"

Her mother looked down and smoothed the front of her dress, picking at a wrinkle no one else could see. Finally, she looked up again, her face smooth and serene. "Actually, it's in England."

It was like someone had dropped a sandbag on Emmy's chest. She couldn't breathe. Boarding school. England. Boarding school. England.

THUMP-thump, THUMP-thump, THUMP-thump.

Clint turned to Emmy. "And how do you feel about all this? It must have been a bit of a shock when you first found out."

Emmy's mom swallowed hard and stared at Emmy like she was begging her to say the right thing.

The room started to spin, like Emmy was on an out-of-control merry-go-round. She managed a wobbly smile. "I'm just happy to support my mother."

Her mom put a steadying hand around Emmy's elbow. "You're just too good to me. Darling, I need to freshen up. Come with me?" She pulled on Emmy's elbow and guided her to the bathroom.

"Okay." Her mom closed the door behind them. "You look faint. You're not going to pass out, are you?"

Emmy fell into a rickety chair in the corner. She didn't know what passing out felt like, but if the room kept spinning, she'd probably end up on the floor. She leaned her head against the wall, and the spinning started to slow down.

"Take a deep breath, and we can talk about this."

Emmy wrapped her arms around her stomach and tried to breathe in, but there didn't seem to be enough air in the room. She wanted to ask questions—and to say how unfair this was—but it felt like someone had stuck a piece of gum inside the part of her brain that formed complete sentences.

Boarding school. England. Boarding school. England.

The words kept running through her head.

"I'm sorry you had to find out this way," her mom said. "I only finalized things with the headmaster this morning, and

I didn't want to tell you until I knew I had your schooling settled. I was going to tell you this afternoon, but that whole stitches debacle took all day."

"Why can't I stay here?" Emmy finally managed to say.

"There's no one to look after you."

"But—"

"Emmy, I am a child psychologist, and I am your mother. I know what's best for you."

Emmy sighed. She'd heard that phrase for almost twelve years, and she still hadn't found a way to argue with it. "When would I have to leave?"

Her mom looked away. "It's a bit of an unusual circumstance. They don't usually allow new students once term has started, so we're really lucky they let you in at all. But I had to agree to send you as soon as possible so you don't miss any more class time."

Emmy's eyes welled up with tears. She was moving to another continent, she was doing it by herself, and she was doing it soon.

"Darling, I know this is difficult, but you're going to need to be strong. There's press out there, and I don't want them to think there might be something wrong. Gretchen is promoting me as a mentor for the moms and dads of America. Think of all the people I'll be able to help. But if you don't seem supportive, that'll be the story, and I won't be nearly as effective. Besides, this is a chance for you to get a top-notch education."

"That's what you said about Bartholomew Prep and Glenmore Heights."

"I know, but both of them really took a tumble in school rankings, and I couldn't leave you there if they weren't going to help you get ahead. This school is going to be different."

That's what her mom always said. Every time a school dropped a few ranks, she got nervous about Emmy not getting a good enough education, as if being at the fourth-best school in New England was worse than being at the second-best. But boarding school? Emmy couldn't even imagine it.

Her mom grabbed her hand and held it steady. "Em, I didn't mean to keep this from you," she said. "I promise we'll talk more later, and then we'll have no more secrets between us."

Emmy thought about her nightstand and the strange letter shut up inside it. The one she'd never tell her mom about, not in a million years. "Right. No more secrets."

CHAPTER 2

The School

Wellsworth is a fabulous school, darling. You're going to love it," her mom said. It was after midnight, and they were driving back home. The last thing Emmy wanted to do was talk. She pressed her head against the car window and pretended to sleep. Her mom didn't take the hint.

"England is amazing. I spent a few years there with my cousin Lucy, and it was one of the best experiences of my life."

Emmy's eyes flew open. *England*. Her mother had gone to England. That's where she had met…

She pursed her lips. The letter with his name had arrived only a few days before. That was way too much of a coincidence. She glanced at her mother. Could she ask about him without raising suspicion?

"Oh right," Emmy said casually. "You met Dad in England, didn't you?"

Her mom cleared her throat. She always did that when Emmy brought up her father. "Yes, I did."

So far, so good.

"You haven't heard anything about him lately, have you?"

"Of course not! He's been gone nine years. Why would anyone hear from him now?"

Images flickered in Emmy's mind like an old home movie: A pair of strong hands lifting her high in the air. A scratchy beard nuzzling her face. The smell of peppermint chewing gum. It had been nine years. Ever since her third birthday when her cake sat uneaten in the fridge. Nobody felt like celebrating.

"Does he still have family in England?"

Her mom stared at the road. Her face, which had been so full of energy and excitement while she was talking about the school, now looked like it had been carved in stone. "Your father didn't have any family."

"Or maybe…friends?" Emmy persisted. "Anyone who knew him well?"

"Why are you asking all these questions about your father?"

Emmy looked at her hands. She didn't want her mom to get suspicious. "I was only curious."

Her mom sighed. "As far as I know, he never had contact with anyone from England after we moved here. I think it's best not to focus on him. It's just you and me now, and that's not so bad, right?"

Emmy looked out the window. "Right." She wasn't sure if she meant it or not, but it seemed like the best way to end the conversation. She needed time to think. And plan.

It wasn't hard to convince her mom she needed to go to bed as soon as they got home. The hard part was making sure that her mom didn't figure out she wasn't planning on sleeping. Emmy quietly pulled her nightstand drawer open and moved all the knickknacks aside. Way at the back, exactly where she'd left it, was the letter. She'd looked at it so many times in

the last three days she had it memorized, but she took it out
and reread it:

> Dear Emmeline,
>   Changes are coming. There's more to your
> father than you realize. If you've found any of his
> relics, keep them safe.
>   Sincerely,
>
>   A friend

Emmy didn't know what to make of it. Changes are coming.
Could this person have known Emmy's mom was sending her
to England? How could that be possible when Emmy hadn't
even known herself? She looked at the letter again. *Her father.*
His relics. But she didn't have anything that belonged to her
father. Her mother had gotten rid of everything he owned
when he disappeared. Yet this "friend" seemed to think Emmy
might have some kind of relics that belonged to him.

She lay on the bed and stared at the ceiling. This house had
been in her mom's family for generations. She'd never sell it.
If her dad wanted to hide something valuable, it would be the
perfect place.

Emmy crept to her door and eased it open. The light in her

mom's bedroom was out. She tiptoed up the little staircase that wound its way around the chimney and unlatched the narrow door that led to the attic. She shuddered in the cold and flicked on the light. There was stuff everywhere: a spinning wheel that must have belonged to a long-lost ancestor, a telephone with a long curly cord that plugged into the wall, even an old desktop computer her mom must have forgotten to get rid of. Any of it could be considered a relic. So, which one belonged to her dad?

She opened the nearest box. It was just old cables. The next three boxes she looked in had receipts and documents that looked like they were for her mom's taxes. The fifth box was filled with more documents, and Emmy was about to close it when a page at the bottom caught her eye. Did that say "marriage"? She pulled the paper out; at the top in huge letters it read, "Marriage Certificate." Emmy swallowed hard and read the names.

Pamela Willick. Thomas Allyn.

Emmy frowned. That couldn't be right. Wasn't her dad's name Willick? The certificate made it look like her dad had taken her mom's last name. She shrugged. He must have been really progressive.

Emmy looked around the room. There had to be more things about her dad up here, things her mom hadn't gotten rid of. She searched every box, but nothing else had her dad's name. A glimmer of daylight started shining through the tiny attic window. Her mom would be waking up any minute. She was running out of time.

She rubbed the goose bumps on her arms and tried to remember what the letter had said. *If you've found any of his relics, keep them safe*. Relics. Documents weren't really relics, and if they were sitting out in the open, that wouldn't be very safe. Maybe there was a hiding spot. She stepped around the ice-cold chimney and rubbed her hands along the walls. Nothing seemed like the latch to a hidden door. She could tap on the floorboards to see if one might be loose, but that would probably wake up her mom. Besides, it was a two-hundred-year-old farmhouse. All the floorboards were loose.

Emmy sighed. It'd be nearly impossible to search for a hiding spot without making a big racket. She put her hand on the great stone chimney and reached for the door, then stopped. Why wasn't this part of the chimney as cold as the rest of it? The texture felt different too, like all the grit had been rubbed off the stone. Emmy looked closer. It had some kind of coating on it, like hard plastic that was made to look like a rock. She reached her fingers around it. There was a groove, one that her fingers fit inside. She yanked and the fake stone flew into her hands, revealing a giant hole behind it. There was a metal box inside.

Emmy's heart started beating harder. This was definitely a relic. She pulled out the box and felt a jolt in her stomach. It was beautiful. There were carvings all around the outside: roses and thorns and intricate crosses. Slowly and carefully, she opened the lid. There was a letter inside:

My dear Pamela, I know you must be upset with me, but if you find these, please don't get rid of them. They're very important.

My dearest Emmeline, if you find these, keep them safe. And I wouldn't tell your mother if I were you.

Love, Tom/Dad

The letter started shaking in Emmy's hand. *My dearest Emmeline. Love Dad.* Her father had written this letter, and he'd written it to her.

She put the letter aside and gasped. Twelve medallions were fitted into slots, and each one was a different shape. Some were round, some were teardrops, and each of them were intricately carved masterpieces. Every groove, every curve, every edge looked like it was exactly where it was meant to be, creating a set where no two medallions were alike. She picked one up and pressed it into the palm of her hand. Were these really her father's? She had never owned anything that belonged to her dad. She had never even *seen* anything that belonged to him.

She sat on the frigid wood floor and put the box on her lap. What should she do with it? The letter had said she should keep her dad's relics safe. Did that mean she should hide them in her room? Or should she take them with her to England? She didn't even know if she wanted to go to England at all. She leaned her head against the wall and sighed. She could refuse to go. She could march down to breakfast and tell her mom she wasn't going anywhere and that was that. But there was this part of her, this tiny voice, that said, *Why not?* What would she be leaving behind? Heating up frozen lasagna while she waited for her mom to get home? Watching reruns alone on a Saturday night?

England. Her Dad's home. Could she find a home there too?

Emmy tapped her fingers on the box. Whoever sent her that letter must have known she was supposed to go to England, and that these medallions were hidden in this house. They must have known about her dad. And if going to England meant the chance to learn more about her father, she was going to take it.

She bit her lip. Now she just had to figure out how to keep her mom from finding out about the letter and medallions before she got on the plane.

A week later she was standing in Heathrow Airport's arrivals hall, trying to navigate a luggage cart through swarms of stressed-out travelers. Somebody from the school was supposed to pick her up, but she had no clue how to recognize the person. Maybe they'd have a sign with Emmy's name on it, like in the movies.

"Excuse me, might you be Emmeline Willick?"

Emmy whirled around. A man with a shaved head and stubbled chin was staring at her. "Uh, yeah, I'm Emmy."

The man held out his hand. "I'm Jonas Tresham, and I'm here to take you to Wellsworth."

Emmy bit her lip. She'd pictured someone prim and proper and wearing a fancy suit. This guy was wearing a black hoodie and looked like he hadn't shaved in a week. "You're from Wellsworth?"

He pointed to a patch on his hoodie. "That's what it says on my paycheck, as well as my jacket."

Emmy squinted at the patch; it said "Wellsworth." She took his outstretched hand and shook it.

"Would you like to wait out front while I bring the car around?" he asked.

"No, I'll just walk." After eight hours of travel, she was desperate to stretch her legs.

It didn't take long to find the Wellsworth car. It looked like something the royal family would ride in: sleek, black, and huge. Jonas didn't just drive fast, he drove *crazy* fast. And he wasn't the only one. Just getting onto the freeway felt like a NASCAR race, but with everyone on the wrong side of the road.

After what seemed like forever on the freeway, the car veered into an exit lane and started to slow down. Soon they were on a new road—a slower road—and Emmy could finally look out the window without getting dizzy. Thick hedges lined the narrow street and almost brushed the side of the car. They turned onto a driveway and went under a heavy stone archway with the word "Wellsworth" carved into the top. Emmy pressed her nose to the window, but there were so many trees that she couldn't catch a glimpse of the school. Finally, they reached the end of the driveway.

She clutched her backpack tightly, clambered out of the car, and looked up. Way up. She'd been to a lot of private schools, but none of them looked like this. It had tall spires and massive arched windows, like the cathedrals in New York City. A maze of walls sprung out in every direction, as if people had just added more rooms when they needed space.

A woman with wild black hair walked down the front stairs, leaning on a cane with every step.

"Emmeline Willick?"

"Yes," Emmy said.

"Welcome to Wellsworth. I'm Madam Boyd. I'll be your housemistress. That means I'm here to support you, offer guidance, and make sure you don't flunk out."

Emmy tried to swallow, but her mouth felt like sandpaper. Was flunking out a likely possibility?

"Let's get you to the house."

Jonas heaved her luggage out of the trunk and the three of them walked down a path that snaked around the side of the sprawling building. As soon as they rounded the corner, the wind just about knocked Emmy off her feet. It bit at her cheeks like an icy whip, as if she'd just walked into a frozen wind tunnel.

"I've been having a look at your school records," Madam Boyd said. "You haven't got any Latin?"

"Uh, no."

"And no Greek?"

"No."

Madam Boyd shook her head. "No classical studies, no literature, and who knows what they've been teaching you in 'U.S. History.' Well, no use flapping about it, we'll just keep the head and deal with it in the morn's morn."

It was like Madam Boyd spoke a different version of English, one with unrecognizable words with extra R's and no G's. Maybe she was from Ireland or Scotland.

"You'll have to start off in a first-year Latin class, and I'll be putting you in the Latin Society to help you catch up," Madam Boyd said.

"What's the Latin Society?"

"A group committed to learning and excelling in Latin studies. They read and discuss Latin literature and offer assistance to students who need extra guidance."

A Latin reading club. That had to be the most boring thing she'd ever heard of. "Are there any other clubs I could join? Like soccer, maybe?"

"You'll find information on all our games and societies, including football, in your school handbook."

Emmy felt a jolt in her chest. So, they *did* have a soccer team. At least there was one thing to look forward to.

Madam Boyd glanced at her. "Latin Society can be a bit...

boisterous. Some of their members have a habit of making poor choices. Nevertheless, they boast some of the highest Latin exam scores in the country, and, given how behind you are, I think it will be a real benefit to you. Just make sure you stay out of trouble."

Emmy nodded, even though she couldn't imagine what kind of trouble she would find at a stuffy old Latin club.

They walked across the blowing grounds until they took a sharp turn into a wall of trees. Wherever they were going, it was well concealed. Madam Boyd took another sharp turn and stopped so abruptly Emmy almost ran into her. There, in a clearing, stood two stone towers that looked like they were hooked onto a large round room that sat between them.

"These are the Edmund and Audrey Houses," Madam Boyd said. "You'll be on the third floor in Audrey—that's the girls' house." She looked at Jonas. "Would you mind bringing Miss Willick's things to her room? I have something to discuss with her before she goes in."

Jonas nodded and brought Emmy's suitcases inside.

Madam Boyd looked squarely at Emmy. "Miss Willick, I must be frank with you. I have some concerns about you being admitted to Wellsworth."

Emmy looked down at her hands.

"Not because you aren't a good student," Madam Boyd went on, "but because of how much pressure this will put on you. You haven't grown up in our school system. You missed all of first and second year, and you've missed the start of third year. Even though there'll be some overlap with your American schooling, you are still incredibly behind. I'm not telling you this to discourage you, but to give you a realistic expectation of the work you have ahead. I explained all this to your mother, but she insisted you could handle it. However, if Wellsworth is too much for you, we can make other arrangements. Do you understand?"

Emmy nodded and tucked her hair behind her ear. School had never been too much for her before, but she'd never been to one like this. Maybe Wellsworth wasn't such a good idea.

"There's a school handbook in your room," Madam Boyd said. "You'll find a map in there along with your timetable. Unfortunately, I have a meeting, so I can't come in with you, but your roommate will help you get settled."

Madam Boyd shook Emmy's hand. "I won't wish you good luck, because with hard work and self-discipline, you won't need it."

Emmy nodded weakly but wished she really did have a good luck charm. It sounded like she was going to need it.

Madam Boyd disappeared into the trees, and Jonas came out of the house. "Everything all right?"

Emmy shrugged. The stitches in her forehead still ached, she'd been traveling forever, and her housemistress didn't think she could hack it.

"If you don't mind my saying, you do look a bit peaky, young miss. Should I fetch someone to come and—"

"I'm fine," Emmy said. She didn't know what *peaky* meant, but it couldn't be good.

Jonas scratched his stubbly chin. "I know Wellsworth can be a bit daunting at first. I was a student here myself. Even though I graduated almost twenty years ago, I still remember that overwhelming feeling. It makes a lot of people wonder whether this is really the place for them."

Emmy's eyes filled with tears. She'd only just gotten there, and she was already so far behind she might never catch up. Maybe she should just get back on the plane and not look back.

"No one's going to make you stay," Jonas said. "Only you can decide if it's worth it."

Emmy hiked her bag a little higher on her shoulder. She could feel the outline of the box inside it, like a talisman that held part of her father—part of herself—inside it. It felt heavy against her back, like it was trying to get her attention. *I'm here*, it was saying, *I'm here. Don't forget about me.*

"Well, you'd best be getting inside," Jonas said. "If you need any help, I'll be around."

"Thanks," Emmy said, and Jonas disappeared into the trees.

Emmy turned and stared at the thick wooden door. It was now or never. She clutched her bag tightly, pushed down on the iron handle, and heaved open the door.

CHAPTER 3

Audrey House

So far everything at Wellsworth had been so cold and quiet that the school seemed practically deserted—but not this room. It was crammed with people, all shouting over the music that blasted off every wall. Heat poured out of a massive double-sided fireplace that snapped and crackled in the middle of the room.

"You can't be serious," someone said. "*Another* accident?"

A boy shook his head. "This is the third time someone from Latin Society's gotten hurt this year."

Latin Society. That was the club she was supposed to join.

"Jumping off a roof isn't an accident. It's just stupid."

Emmy stopped walking. Somebody jumped off a roof? That wasn't stupid; more like insane.

"Maybe they'll finally get in trouble."

The other boy rolled his eyes. "Not a chance. Those guys can weasel out of anything."

They started talking about rugby, which Emmy didn't know a thing about. She looked around; where was she supposed to go? There were two staircases, one on each side of the room, and each of them had a giant banner hanging beside it. The one on the left was deep blue and had the name "Audrey" stitched in scrawling letters. Hopefully that meant she'd find the girls' rooms over there.

The third floor was dark and musty, like someone had spritzed old dust piles with hair spray. There were nameplates on every door: *Natalie Walsh and Jeannette Beauguin. Lola Boyd and Arabella Gray. Fenella Greenborough and Jaya Singh. Victoria Stuart-Bevington and Emmeline Willick.* Emmy wiped her sweaty palm on her jeans, turned the door handle, and walked into her room.

She frowned. *Was* this her room? Every inch of it was covered in stuff. Picture frames, knickknacks, and heaps of clothes that had been drenched in overpowering perfume. There wasn't even space to sit down on one of the beds. She opened the closets. Both were crammed full. Her suitcases were in front of one of the beds, but it looked like two girls already lived here. There must have been some kind of mistake, and she didn't even know who to ask to fix it.

The door burst open, and a girl stormed in, slamming the door behind her. She walked straight past Emmy, her blond ponytail bouncing behind her, and she pulled a large roll of yellow tape out of one of the desk drawers.

Emmy twisted her fingers behind her back. She should introduce herself. Or at least say hi. Or just run out the door and never come back. "Uh, hi? I'm Emmy Wi—"

"Don't talk to me," the girl snapped. She bent down and put a long line of tape on the floor. "I hear you've never been to a boarding school before. First rule: stay out of your roommate's space. Since you're new, I thought I would make that part easy for you." She pointed a bony finger to one side of the room. "Everything on this side of the tape is mine. Everything else is your half."

Emmy frowned. Her "half" was about a quarter of the size of the other girl's.

"Second rule: stay out of your roommate's stuff." The girl threw the tape back in the drawer. "If I catch you looking inside my closets, I'll get you expelled for stealing."

"But where—"

"You've got suitcases. If they're big enough to hold your rubbish now, they'll be big enough all year."

"All right." Emmy gritted her teeth. "I'm Emmy Willick." She held out her hand, and the girl looked at it as if it were a dirty sock.

"Let's get one thing straight. When I started the year, that door only had one name on it: mine. Victoria Stuart-Bevington. I wasn't supposed to have a roommate this year. As far as I'm concerned, I still don't have a roommate this year." She wrenched the door open and marched out, pulling off Emmy's nameplate as she went.

Emmy shoved a pile of clothes off the bed and threw herself down. Well, this was lovely.

Emmy heard lots of voices floating up and down the hallway, but she didn't see anyone else that afternoon. By the time five thirty rolled around, she figured it must be dinnertime, even if her jet-lagged stomach didn't agree. She flipped through the school handbook until she found a section called Dining. Apparently, everyone ate in a room called the Hall, which was actually an old cathedral that the school had renovated. That must be why the school reminded her of a church. It used to be one.

The Hall was part of the main building, and Emmy didn't need the handbook's map to find it. As soon as she got close, she heard voices and cutlery echoing off every stone wall. She grabbed a few things off the food table and sat in the quietest corner.

After dinner she came back to an empty dorm room. She could go down to the common room and try to make some friends, but what was the point? She'd just say the wrong thing. Besides, Wellsworth wasn't the first school her mom had sent her to so she could get a "top-notch education," and it probably wouldn't be the last. She'd figured out a long time ago that friends never stuck around when she switched schools, so why bother making new ones?

She started rummaging for her pajamas and found her soccer cleats instead. Maybe soccer might give her a friend or two. She'd never fit in on her teams at home because she always played with older girls, but that might be different here. Then again, she might not even make the team.

She sighed and pulled out her father's box. Had he ever been to a school like this in England? Had he made friends easily? Emmy's mom was always so bubbly, like some kind of delicious drink, but Emmy…well, she was more like a soda can that had gone flat. Maybe she was more like her dad. Or maybe she was just an anomaly. An evolutionary blip that would disappear as quickly as she had come.

She slid the box under her bed—Victoria didn't seem like the kind of roommate who would understand about her dad. She opened up her laptop and typed "Thomas Allyn" into her web browser. She'd searched for her dad a thousand times, but she'd never found anything. This time was no different.

She closed her laptop and slipped it back into its case. There must be a reason someone had sent her that letter now, right before she got to England, but she had no clue how to figure that reason out. How could she find information about someone who seemed to have been erased?

Emmy jumped. Her cell phone was ringing. She pulled it out of her backpack. "Hello?"

"Hello, darling!" her mother said. "How are you? Did you have a good flight?"

"Yeah, it was fine."

"How are you getting settled in? Have you met your roommate? Are you making lots of friends already?"

"Uh…"

"Never mind, I guess you just got there, but I'm sure friends will come easily enough."

Emmy didn't say anything. When had she ever made friends easily?

"Listen, darling, I can't talk long, I'm having dinner with Gretchen, but there was one tiny thing we didn't get to discuss before you left."

Emmy's whole body got stiff. Any time her mother said they had to talk about something, it rarely turned out to be tiny.

"Wellsworth has very challenging academic standards, and I think it's best if you don't take on any extracurricular activities that aren't directly related to your studies."

"What do you mean?"

Her mother cleared her throat. "I think it's best if you focus on schoolwork. You can't afford to be distracted by anything extra, like clubs, or sports, or—"

"You mean soccer." Emmy's heart hammered against her ribs. "You're saying I'm not allowed to play soccer."

"That's right."

Emmy's voice seemed to have disappeared. She had a million things to say, but she couldn't spit any of them out.

"I know that might be a bit disappointing, but—"

"Disappointing!?" Emmy blurted. "Soccer's one of the most important things in my life, Mom! You can't just take that away from me!"

"Emmy, don't be so dramatic. I know soccer is important to you, but it's just a game. You're almost twelve; you need to start focusing on what really matters. These next few years of school will shape the course of your life. You can't afford to be distracted."

"It's never been a problem before."

"But now you're at a much more rigorous school. It's not like we can move you somewhere else if you run into trouble."

"But Madam Boyd said I could go somewhere else if Wellsworth was too hard."

"Emmeline, do you have any idea how humiliating it would be if you had to leave school?"

"You've moved me to new schools before."

"Yes, but boarding school is different." She paused and took a deep breath. "I was doing an interview yesterday, and the reporter asked whether sending you to a boarding school showed good parenting skills. I have to be careful about this.

Can you imagine how damaging it would be to my career if I sent my daughter to boarding school and she couldn't cope? The press would have a field day with me, with both of us."

Emmy's jaw went tight. So that's what this was really about. Her mom's career. It was always about her mom's career.

Her mom sighed. "We'll have to finish this conversation later, I'm going to be late. I love you." The phone went dead.

Emmy clicked the red button on her phone. No soccer. The one thing she was looking forward to. The one thing that mattered. The one place *Emmy* mattered. But that didn't matter to her mother.

Emmy hadn't been asleep that long when her alarm started blaring the next morning. She rubbed her eyes. Victoria was nowhere to be seen. *Probably got up early so I couldn't ask her for help.*

Emmy's school uniform wouldn't be ready for a few days, but she had a gray skirt and a sage green sweater that might blend in. Her first two classes were economics and biology, and they were every bit as hard as Madam Boyd had warned. The economics teacher kept sneezing, which made him lose his train of thought and change topics in the middle of a sentence. After class he dumped a stack of homework sheets on Emmy's desk and walked away before she could ask any questions. The biology teacher was more helpful, but he spent so long going on about natterjack toads that she missed lunch. When the bell rang, she had to race to her fine arts class, where she was bowled over by the smell of moldy fruit.

"We need to sketch the fruit in various states of decay," the teacher drawled. "It draws us closer to the very essence of the peach!"

After madly taking notes on oil spills in geography, she checked her after-school schedule. She was supposed to talk about a plan for learning Latin with a teacher named Master Larraby. She followed the map to the Classical Studies wing, found the right office, and waited. And waited. And waited. She checked her schedule again. *Latin tutorial, Master Larraby's office, Classical Studies department.* She was definitely in the right place, but there was no teacher to be found.

An hour later, she threw her bag over her shoulder and stomped back down the hallway. What a waste of time. At least if she went back to her room, she could get a little homework done before dinner.

She slipped into the common room and nearly bumped into

a group of girls who were crowded around a fancy-looking shoebox.

"Where did you get them, Jaya?" an older girl asked.

"Mum just sent them from Milan," answered a willowy girl with dark hair and eyes. "I hope they fit; she never gets my size right. She's so self-involved, it's like she forgets who I am."

"That's nothing," said another girl. "When I turned fifteen, my mum sent me a 'Happy Seventeenth' card and gave me a car."

"Did you hear about Malcolm Galt?" said the girl called Jaya. "He jumped off the chapter house and broke his arm."

Somebody laughed. "What else is new? He never could resist a dare."

"I hear Dev Masrani was there, too," an older girl said. "He's still in the medical center."

Jaya's jaw dropped. "Is he hurt badly?"

"I don't know," the girl said. "He didn't go to the hospital, so I guess it can't be that bad."

"Then why is he still in the medical center?"

The girl shrugged. "Beats me."

Emmy slid past the girls and ducked her head. People were starting to stare.

"Has anybody talked to her yet?" someone whispered.

"How did she get in after term started?"

"Maybe she has famous parents."

"I bet they just sent her with a big fat donation."

"Honestly," said a black-haired girl on the couch, "if you want to know who she is, why don't you bloody well ask her?" She jumped up, marched over to Emmy, and stuck out her hand. She was shorter than Emmy, but her handshake was so powerful it made Emmy wince. "I'm Lola Boyd. Who are you?"

"Uh, Emmy Willick."

"Good, then," Lola said. "Now, do you want to sit with us or would you rather stand here and feel like an idiot?"

Emmy had no clue what to say to that. At least Lola was talking to her. Lola had been sitting with a boy who was fiddling with a music player. He had dark eyes and skin, and everything about him was messy—his hair, his shirt, even his tie. Then he looked up and smiled. It was the first smile Emmy had seen in two days. She tucked her hair behind her ear and sat down.

Lola slumped down on the couch and threw her feet up on the coffee table, her thick black boots clunking heavily on the wood. Emmy smiled. Those boots definitely weren't part of the uniform code. Lola had an accent, too, and this time Emmy was pretty sure it was Scottish.

"Don't worry about those gossiping harpies," Lola said. "Their barks are worse than their bites."

"I'm Jack." The boy pulled out one of his ear buds. "Jack Galt."

Galt. Like the boy who had broken his arm. Maybe they were related.

"I'm Emmy Willick."

"Wow, American," Jack said. "We don't get a lot of you at Wellsworth. Parents scarpered, have they?"

Emmy blinked. "Huh?"

Jack shook his head and smiled. "It means they took off and left you here. You've never been to a school in the UK, have you?"

Emmy shook her head.

A group of older boys walked past them, laughing and talking loudly. One of them had his arm in a cast. Jack's whole body went stiff.

"Have you talked to him yet?" Lola asked.

"Nope."

"Are you going to?"

Jack shrugged. "What's there to say?"

"I don't know, maybe, 'Sorry you broke your arm while you were being a stupid show-off, Malcolm. Hope it doesn't hurt too much.'"

The boy laughed while he tried to balance a stack of books on his cast. He looked a lot older, probably in his last year at school. "Is that the kid who jumped off the roof?"

"Something like that," Jack said. "That's my brother, Malcolm."

Emmy looked back at the boy. His skin and hair were so much lighter than Jack's. It was hard to believe they shared the same DNA. "He doesn't really, um, I mean, you don't exactly look alike."

"Yeah, everyone says that. My dad's white, and Malcolm takes after him. I look a lot more like my mum—she's from Sri Lanka."

"Is Dev still in the medical center?" Lola asked.

Jack nodded. "I don't think he's too badly hurt, just shaken up. I went to see him this morning."

"What was he doing with Malcolm?"

Jack rolled his eyes. "Latin Society."

"Jeez, can't they get those Latin Society blokes under control? They think they're bloody invincible, and then somebody ends up in the medical center for two days."

Emmy rubbed her fingers together. She wasn't sure she wanted to be part of this Latin Society.

"Can't the principal do anything about it?" she asked.

"Principal?" Lola said. "You mean the headmaster?"

Emmy nodded.

"We don't see him much. He's always busy with teachers or

40

school governors. The housemasters and housemistresses are the ones who really run things. It was probably the same at your old school."

"We didn't have housemasters or housemistresses at my old school."

"No?" Lola picked up a soccer magazine. "Who took care of the boarders?"

"I didn't go to a boarding school. I lived at home with my mom."

Lola raised her eyebrows.

"You've never been a boarder?" Jack asked.

Emmy shook her head. Jack and Lola looked at each other.

"What?" Emmy's chest was tightening up again. "Is it really that bad?"

Lola shrugged. "Depends."

"On what?"

"On lots of things." Suddenly Lola slammed her magazine shut and stared at Emmy. "Wait, who's your roommate?"

"Some girl named Victoria."

Jack groaned, and Lola winced. She shook her head and opened her magazine again. "They're not even giving you a fighting chance."

CHAPTER 4

Humanities and Latin

The next day's classes were just as hard, and the jet lag wasn't helping. She was late for two classes, which earned her some pretty good glares from the teachers. She ducked down a flight of rickety steps that were supposed to lead to the Howard Room for her last class of the day: humanities.

She paused. Was she in the right place? It looked way older than the rest of the school. It had a dank, musty smell, like no one had opened a window in years. Actually, there were no windows at all. Just flickering light bulbs and the occasional security camera. The ceiling was held up with wooden beams that hung so low a tall person might have to duck.

The hallway meandered a long way. The sound of voices echoed around a corner, and they finally led her to the Howard Room. She shoved the heavy door open and blinked. This was no ordinary classroom. It was a perfect circle lined with round benches. A steep stone staircase led down to a scuffed platform where a teacher might give lectures. It was like being at one of those old colleges—like Harvard or Yale. Emmy swallowed hard. Even the classroom felt way over her head.

She slid into a bench at the back, and someone cleared her throat. "You're in my seat."

Emmy turned around. Victoria was sneering at her, along with another girl who smirked like a cat that had seen a mouse.

"Sorry." Emmy picked up her bag. "I didn't know these seats were assigned."

"They're not." A man strode into the room carrying a stack of books and papers. "And as such, I'm sure Miss Stuart-Bevington would be more than happy to find her own seat rather than usurping someone else's."

Victoria flashed a tight smile, like she was supposed to be

happy about eating lima beans. Emmy cringed. She would pay for this later.

"Uh, that's okay, I don't mind," Emmy said, "I'll just—"

"Miss Stuart-Bevington and Miss Gray could do with a change of scenery," the man said. "I think their recent quiz results suggest that a trip to the front row would do them a world of good."

Victoria pressed her lips together. "No problem," she said in an ultrasweet voice. "Come on, Arabella." The two girls grumbled all the way down to the front row.

"You must be Emmeline," the man said.

"It's Emmy."

"Nice to meet you, Emmy. I'm John Barlowe. I assume you've never taken a humanities class before?"

Emmy shook her head.

"Not to worry, we'll get you sorted out."

He turned and stepped lightly down the steps to the platform below. Lola and Jack came racing through the door and squeezed next to Emmy just as the second bell rang.

"Nicely done," Lola commended. "How'd you get the harpies out of the back row?"

"Very brave for your second day," Jack leaned closer and whispered, "I wouldn't have had the guts."

"All right, let's get started." Master Barlowe didn't have to say it very loudly. His voice bounced off the old wood and stone like it was magnified by magic.

"Now that we've finished our introductory unit, we can start delving into British history and culture. In your first two years, you should have covered the Roman period, the Anglo-Saxons, and the Plantagenets. Today we start examining the Tudor period."

Emmy stifled a groan. She didn't even know who the Plant-ee-geniuses were, let alone how they fit into British history.

"I should warn you," Master Barlowe continued, "the Tudor period is not for the faint of heart. It was marked by intrigue, betrayal, and terrible violence. Monarchs were assassinated, people were murdered because of their religions, and women had absolutely no legal rights. And yet, at the same time, public education was born and some of the most beautiful pieces of English literature were penned."

Emmy sat up a little straighter. She was used to spending history lessons memorizing names and dates, but Barlowe made it sound like this class might be interesting.

"It was a time of great contradiction, and as you will see, many of the most important things that happened were carried out in secret. Secret marriages, secret alliances, and secret plots that led to the undoing of Britain's most powerful men and women."

Emmy shifted in her seat. Something about what Barlowe was saying didn't make sense, but it was only her first day. If she asked a question, she'd probably just look stupid.

"Why are you all wiggly?" Lola hissed. "Do you have to use the loo or something?"

Emmy just about choked. "No! I just…it's nothing. I just had a question."

"So, ask it."

"No!"

"Why not?"

"I—"

"Is there something you ladies wish to add?"

Emmy sank low into the bench. Barlowe was looking straight at her and Lola.

Lola smirked. "Emmy has a question."

Emmy groaned. Maybe being friends with Lola wasn't such a good idea.

"Yes, Miss Willick?"

Emmy cleared her throat. "I was just wondering—"

"I'm sorry, Master Barlowe," Victoria interrupted, "I can't hear her down here. Can you get her to talk louder please?"

Victoria's friend smothered a giggle. Victoria was just trying to make Emmy even more uncomfortable.

Emmy tucked her hair behind her ear. *Jeez, why does she hate me so much? She doesn't even know me.*

Master Barlowe smiled. "Miss Willick, could you speak up a little?"

Emmy nodded. "I was just wondering about how you said women had no legal rights."

"That's correct."

"But then you said there were powerful women. How could women be powerful if they had no legal rights?"

Master Barlowe folded his hands behind his back and walked a few paces. "That is a very interesting question. It is true that women had few legal rights during the Tudor period. But that doesn't mean they couldn't influence the men who *did* have legal rights. Have any of you heard of Anne Boleyn?"

Nobody said anything. Emmy had heard the name before, but she didn't know where.

Lola put her hand in the air. "She was a queen who got her head hacked off."

Emmy winced. Lola definitely had a way with words.

"Succinctly put," Barlowe said. "Anne Boleyn was the second wife of King Henry the Eighth, and yes, she was beheaded. Beheadings are a common theme of the Tudor period. But it is her life, rather than her death, that we are interested in. As a woman, she had no legal rights in Britain. However, the events surrounding her life literally changed the course of history.

"As influential as she was, much of her life was carried out in secret. She secretly married King Henry while he was technically married to another woman. She secretly tried to influence the king's closest advisers. And because of her influence, people secretly plotted to have her tried and convicted of treason for a crime she did not commit."

Emmy leaned her chin on her hand. It sounded like Anne had gotten caught up in *other* people's secrets. Those secrets weren't worth killing her, were they?

Barlowe stopped pacing. "Now, now, we're getting ahead of ourselves. Let's go back a little earlier and talk about the War of the Roses."

As jet-lagged as she was, Emmy had no trouble staying awake in this class. Barlowe was animated, engaging, and witty. It was nothing like her history classes at home.

While everyone else packed up, Master Barlowe brought Emmy a book titled *How to Destroy a Dynasty: Lessons from the Tudors and Stuarts*.

"Here's the text we are using this term," he said. "I would imagine the only British history you've studied is the part where your ancestors kicked us out of the colonies and said they would no longer listen to our king?"

Emmy bit her lip and nodded.

"Don't worry," Barlowe reassured her. "We'll have you up to speed by the time your General Certificate Exam rolls around in fifth year. I'll talk to Madam Boyd, and we'll come up with a plan to get you on track. And we'll try to make it as painless as possible."

"Master Barlowe," Jack said, "should I take Dev his homework?"

Barlowe frowned. "Unfortunately, Mr. Masrani is no longer a student here."

Jack's jaw dropped. "He left?"

"His parents picked him up this morning."

"But why?"

"I'm afraid I don't know much more than that," Barlowe said. "I'm sorry."

Jack looked worried, and Emmy didn't blame him. Whatever happened on the chapter house roof must have been pretty serious if it made someone leave the school.

Emmy, Jack, and Lola slid out of their bench and walked toward the door, but Lola turned back.

"Yes, Miss Boyd?" Barlowe asked.

"Is what you were saying really true?" Lola asked. "About everyone in the Tudor period keeping secrets?"

"Everyone has secrets, Miss Boyd," he said as he ambled down the stairs. "Some people are just better at hiding them than others."

Brown and orange leaves crunched under Emmy's feet as she made her way to Latin Society. The things Barlowe had said about secrets were really sticking in her mind. Was it true that everyone had secrets? Not just little secrets, but *big* ones, secrets that changed people's lives? She didn't have any secrets like that. Other than the box hiding under her bed. But that wasn't a really *big* secret, was it?

Emmy looked at her map again. She'd better pay attention if she was going to find this place. The Latin Society had its own building called the Lighthouse, which seemed to be in the middle of nowhere. None of the pathways were marked, and she kept running into dead ends where the path just randomly stopped.

After wandering through a garden for a while, Emmy finally found a small stone hut. It had a steep roof, no windows—and no door. They must not expect a lot of visitors.

Emmy walked around the hut a few more times. Still no door. She could be out here forever, and she'd never figure this out.

Crunch, crunch, crunch. Someone was coming down the path. A dark-haired boy came around the corner. He looked familiar—Emmy thought he might be in Edmund House—and she smiled at him. He didn't smile back. He didn't even look at her. He brushed straight past her like she wasn't even there and disappeared around the back of the cottage.

Emmy hesitated for a minute, then followed him. She hurried to the back of the cottage, but by the time she got there, the boy was gone. She put her hands on her hips and stared. There *had* to be an entrance she hadn't noticed. The hut was made of stone and was surrounded by purple flowers, probably lavender. She frowned. There was one sparse patch in the flower bed, bare except for a plant with long sharp leaves that grew tall out of the ground like a guard. She squinted at it. If it looked like a guard, it might be protecting something. Something like a secret entrance. She stepped into the bare patch and peered around the menacing plant. An image, worn and faded, was stamped into the wall. It looked like a skull with something on either side, but she couldn't make out what it was.

Emmy scratched her cheek. It was strange; somehow it

reminded her of something. But that was impossible. She'd never seen anything like this in Connecticut. She carefully reached around the hairy red stalk and tried brushing some dirt off the symbol.

CRACK!

The skull shrank back into the wall, and a gap appeared between two stones. She squeezed her fingers inside it and pulled. The wall swung open.

There were a lot of people crammed into the cottage, and all of them were talking about things she didn't understand.

"Don't be a prat, Asher, you can't talk about Cicero's philosophy without talking about his politics," someone said.

"I'm just saying his writings are strong enough on their own," another responded.

It was like she had walked into another world, one where teenagers thought Latin was fascinating. Emmy pulled the hidden door closed and spotted the dark-haired boy. He was talking to a man who wore a sleek black suit and the shiniest shoes Emmy had ever seen. He did a double take when he saw her, and he whispered something to the dark-haired boy.

"I see we have a new student!" The man smiled at Emmy. "And who might you be?"

Emmy tugged on the sleeve of her sweater. "Um, I'm

Emmy, I mean, Emmeline Willick. Madam Boyd said she'd signed me up for Latin Society."

"Ah yes, I think she mentioned something about that. So sorry, I had meant to leave a guide out there to show you how to get in. You figured it out all right?"

"Eventually." Emmy glanced at the boy. He lifted his chin and sniffed, like someone was serving him brussels sprouts. Then he scowled and walked away. Emmy raised an eyebrow. *Nice guy*.

"I'm Master Larraby," the man said, "and I am the head of Latin Society."

Larraby. So, this was the teacher who had left her sitting in the hallway for an hour the day before.

"We're working in discussion groups today, but I don't think you're quite ready to debate the finer points of Roman politics. Why don't you use this opportunity to catch up on some of your homework?"

Emmy found a quiet corner and opened her Humanities text, sneaking a few peeks around the room. Nobody seemed to have even noticed her. They were all talking and laughing like Latin was the most fascinating subject in the world. The mean dark-haired boy was sitting with Jack's brother, who didn't seem too bothered by his broken arm. He was leaning on the arm of a leather chair, gesturing wildly like he might have been recounting an adventure. Maybe breaking his arm *had* been an adventure. He sounded like a bit of a daredevil. But it wasn't an adventure for the other boy, the one who had left school. Emmy looked around the room. No one seemed shaken up by what had happened to one of their own members.

Then Emmy noticed something else: she was the only girl in the room. That didn't seem right. If so many boys found Latin this interesting, there must be girls who liked it, too.

Emmy started reading and got through a whole chapter by the end of the session. No blaring music, no one yakking on their cell phone, and no Victoria. It was actually a pretty good place to get work done.

The room started emptying out, and Emmy followed the crowd. The bookshelves by the door were crammed full of old books with beautiful leather spines. She cocked her head. One of the spines had the same strange symbol as the hidden door, but this time she could see it much better: a skull with a cross on the right and a dagger on the left. She still had a nagging feeling about it. What did it remind her of? Maybe it was a common symbol in Britain, and her dad had something like it when she was little. It *did* make her think of him. It would be so much easier if she could just ask him stuff like this. She reached for the book. Maybe something inside would trigger her memory.

"Emmeline!" Master Larraby had appeared out of nowhere. "How did you enjoy your time with us? I suppose you found it a bit dull, didn't you?"

Emmy slid the book back in its place. "Actually, I—"

"Not to worry, I won't ask you to suffer through another meeting if it's not really your thing. We'll just switch you to something a little more up your alley. Tell me, are you fond of the noble game of conkers?"

"Uh…"

"I hear they're expecting a visit from the Annapolis Royal Conkers Club this year. Should be very exciting!"

"Actually, I'd like to stay in Latin Society. I could use the extra time to catch up, and it'd be nice to have a teacher around to help me if I get stuck."

"Oh…oh yes, I see." Larraby was smiling, but he didn't look happy. More like confused. "We'll be glad to have you. Now, allow me to show you the way out."

Emmy followed him out the secret door. He didn't seem all that happy about her coming to Latin Society, but that couldn't be right. Why would a teacher not want someone in his club?

CHAPTER 5

Saturday

Emmy got lost twice on her way back to Audrey House, but she eventually found the right path. She slid into the crowded common room and made a beeline for the stairs. She didn't feel like being stared at again.

"Hey, Emmy!" Lola waved at her and pointed to the empty seat at her table. She was sitting with Jack and a few other people Emmy didn't know.

Emmy fiddled with a button on her sweater. She wasn't

really used to people asking her to sit with them. She squeezed in next to Lola and tried to look like she belonged. A girl with blond curls gave Emmy a shy wave, and Emmy waved back.

"That's Natalie," Lola said, "and that's Jaya." She pointed to the willowy girl who had gotten the shoes from her mother. "She's a lot cooler than the rest of us, but we try not to hold that against her."

Emmy blinked. She didn't know what she'd do if someone said that about her. But the girl named Jaya just laughed and went back to her conversation with Natalie.

"Did you have a society today?" Lola asked Emmy.

"Yeah, Latin."

Jack looked up. "You're in the Latin Society?"

"Yeah. Madam Boyd put me in there to try and help me catch up."

"Right." Jack picked up a new pencil and started shading a drawing he was working on. "So how was it? Did you figure out how to get in the building?"

Emmy stared at Jack. How did he know she'd have trouble? "Yeah, but it took a while. Larraby said he'd forgotten to send someone to show me how to get in."

Jack smirked. "He always says that. It's a test. To see if you've got problem-solving skills or something like that."

"Why would you need to pass a test to join a school club?"

"They just want to have more control over who gets in. They're not exactly the friendliest bunch."

"Tell me about it," Emmy grumbled. "There was this one guy who showed up while I was trying to figure out how to get in, and he just pretended I wasn't even there. I think I've seen him around the common room. He must be in Edmund House."

Jack and Lola looked at each other. "Dark hair?" Lola asked.

Emmy nodded.

"Too much hair gel, pretty-boy blazer, looks like he's got a giant stick up his—"

Jack kicked Lola under the table, and she swore.

"That's Brynn, he's Lola's cousin," Jack said. "He was my roommate in first year. Made my life miserable."

"What did he do?"

Jack shifted in his chair. "Mostly pranks, stupid stuff like that."

"It wasn't just 'stupid stuff,'" Lola said. "That night when you—"

"That was an accident," Jack said.

Lola didn't say anything, but it looked like she was practically chewing her tongue to try and keep quiet.

Pranks. Stupid stuff. Accidents. Seemed like Emmy

couldn't hear anything about Latin Society without hearing about those things, too.

"Brynn mostly leaves me alone now," Jack said. "He's too scared of Lola."

Emmy's eyebrows shot up. "Why, what'd you do?"

"She gave him a bloody nose and made him cry in front of all his friends."

Emmy laughed. "You actually punched your cousin?"

"It was good for him," Lola said.

"What did your mom say?"

"I got in massive trouble, but that's nothing new. She didn't care about it being my cousin, though. His dad's my mum's half-brother, but he and my mum don't get on."

"What about your dad?" Emmy asked.

"He lives in Glasgow," Lola replied. "They got divorced when I was one."

"I'm sorry."

Lola shrugged. "Could be worse." She glanced at Jack. He was staring at his fingertips and pinching them together.

"You mean me?" Jack didn't look up. He smiled, but it wasn't a happy smile. "Let's just say I don't exactly fit the Galt family mold. My brothers live up to family expectations better than I ever will."

"How many brothers do you have?" Emmy asked.

"Three. Vincent's already left school; he works for my dad. Oliver won't start here until next year, and Malcolm's in his last year. You probably saw him at Latin Society."

Emmy nodded. She wasn't sure if she should say more. It seemed like Jack's brothers were a bit of a sore spot. "Are there other school societies?"

"Yeah, loads," Lola said. "Jack does all the artsy ones—painting, sculpture, all that junk."

Jack laughed. "While you do all the useless ones like rowing and football."

"Football? You mean soccer?" Finally, a club Emmy could get excited about.

"No, I mean *football*," Lola said, "and you'd better get used to calling it that around here. I'm an attacking midfielder."

Jack snorted. "Yeah, well, I think you took your role as an 'attacker' a bit too seriously last year."

"Why, what did you do?" Emmy asked.

Lola rolled her eyes. "It was no big deal."

"Oh, are you talking about Lola's suspension?" Natalie looked over at them. "I was on the pitch when it happened. She punched a girl in the middle of a match and got herself banned for most of last season. It's practically a school legend."

"It wasn't my fault!" Lola protested.

"How is it not your fault when you punch someone in the face?" Jaya asked.

"That girl was making fun of Mariam's hijab. She's Muslim, and she likes to keep her head covered when she plays. What else was I supposed to do?"

"I don't know, but I probably wouldn't have started a punch-up in front of the official," Jack replied.

"Do you have much football in America, Emmy?" Natalie asked.

"Yeah, there's lots! I mean, our professional league isn't as popular as some other sports, but lots of people play soccer—I mean, football."

"You should come and watch us on Saturday," Natalie said. "The whole school usually comes to our matches."

Emmy's smile faded. Her mom probably wouldn't like her going to a soccer match. "I don't know. I've got a lot of homework."

"Who cares about homework when we're playing Saint Mary's?" Lola asked. "They beat us for the East Anglian Championships last year—we've been waiting to play them for six months!"

Emmy tugged on her ear. Her mother hadn't said she

couldn't *attend* matches. "Well…I guess I could take few hours off from studying."

The others kept talking about the match, but Emmy wasn't listening. She drummed her fingers on the table. What her mother didn't know wouldn't hurt her.

Three days later, Emmy tossed her laundry in a washing machine and looked at her watch. She'd have to hurry if she was going to eat before the match started. She ran upstairs, threw on a sweatshirt, and was almost out the door when she grimaced. There was a lot of homework piled up on her night-stand. She should probably stay in and get some work done. Thanks to Victoria and her irritating friend Arabella, Emmy had hardly gotten anything done all week. They constantly played annoying music, and their nail polish smelled so bad it was like living in the school's chemistry lab.

As aggravating as Victoria was, Emmy's research on her dad was even more frustrating. She was getting nowhere. Anytime she had a moment alone, she'd grab the letter and the box and examine every inch of them. If there was a clue to what those medallions were for, or who had sent the letter, she couldn't figure it out. She didn't know what to do next.

Emmy looked at the homework pile again. If her mom knew she was going to a soccer match when she had so much work to do…

She squared her shoulders and ran out the door. Her mother wasn't here, and she'd get to it later.

She ran into the Hall and started piling food onto a plate. The tables nearby were strangely quiet. The talk about the accident had died down by now, but there was always something that kept people buzzing. Usually everyone was talking over each other, but there was a lot of whispering today. She looked up and her mouth fell open. Half the room was staring at her. Her face got hot and she looked down at her toast. How had she screwed up now?

Jack and Lola were sitting near the door, and Emmy made a beeline for them. Lola looked up and choked, spewing her orange juice across the table.

"What the bloody hell are you wearing!?" she spluttered.

Emmy looked down at her clothes. Blue sweatshirt. Jeans. Old sneakers. Wasn't that good enough for weekends at Wellsworth?

Jack stared at her, a sausage hanging limply from his fork. "You. Cannot. Wear. That. Today."

Emmy pulled at her sweatshirt and sat down. "I thought we didn't have to wear our uniforms on weekends."

"Your uniform would be better than that," Lola scoffed.

"Why, what—"

"You're dressed head to toe in blue," Jack said. "Blue is Saint Mary's color. You look like you're supporting them."

Emmy looked around the Hall. Everyone was wearing Wellsworth's official colors of green and gray. She started chewing her nails. There were so many unwritten rules at this school, she'd never keep them all straight. "I don't have anything green or gray left. I threw it all in the laundry, because I've been wearing it all week."

Jack turned around. "Jaya! Emmy needs some emergency Wellsworth kits. Think you can help?"

Jaya looked Emmy up and down and jumped out of her seat. "No time for breakfast, let's get a move on!"

Twenty minutes later, Emmy was tugging on the cowl of a delicate cashmere sweater. Overflowing sodas and vinegar-soaked fries were being passed all around her in the football stands. *Please don't let me spill on this thing*. The sweater was beautiful, but somehow it made her feel even more plain than usual. Cashmere belonged on girls like Jaya: tall, thin, and chic.

Emmy had to roll up the cuffs on Jaya's slacks, which seriously lessened their sophistication.

Finally, she spotted Jack waving at her, and she eased her way toward him and his friends. A sandy-haired boy leaned down from the row behind and gave her a friendly smile. "It's Emmy, right?"

She nodded.

"I'm Cadel," he said, "I'm Jack's roommate."

Emmy tried to smile. This was one of those times when she was supposed to say something friendly but couldn't figure out what it was.

"I expect you didn't see much football in America," he went on. "Have you ever been to a match before?"

Emmy grinned. "Um, yeah."

"Well, if you have any questions about how it all works, just ask. I play on the boys' team, you know. Made it all the way to the East Anglian Finals last year. Now, there are ten players on the field, excluding the keeper, of course, and—" Cadel was interrupted by the roar of the crowd; the teams had taken the pitch.

"Here, have some licorice." Jack handed her some candy.

"Thanks, but I don't really like licorice."

Jack shoved it into her hand anyway. "Doesn't matter, it's good luck."

Emmy ripped a piece off and dutifully chomped on it as the opening whistle blew.

The game was tense from the very first moments. Both teams were as good as any Emmy had played, and they obviously didn't like each other. The atmosphere in the stands was electric, like the best matches she'd played back home. For the first time since she'd gotten here, something felt familiar: players yelling signals to each other, coaches screaming instructions, the scraping of cleats against grass and rubber. It was like getting a letter from home, one that was bitter and sweet at the same time. She didn't belong in the stands; she belonged on the field. *She* should be the one calling out signals. It should be *her* cleats pounding the turf. When the Wellsworth striker scored in the eightieth minute, Emmy jumped up and down with the rest of the crowd, but she couldn't help wishing she could do more than cheer.

It took a while for the crowd to file out after the match, which gave Cadel a lot of time to explain the game's finer points. "You see, that St. Mary's girl was offside because she was in front of the last defender when her midfielder passed her the ball. Her protest was totally unnecessary. I thought she…"

Somebody bumped into Jack and he grabbed on to Cadel

so he wouldn't fall. Then someone else bumped into Jack, and then a third person. All three boys snickered and kept walking up the stairs like nothing had happened.

"You okay?" Cadel asked.

Jack ran his fingers through his hair. "Yeah, no big deal." His voice cracked a little and he cleared his throat.

"What was that about?" Emmy asked.

"Just a few blokes who don't like me that much."

Emmy looked at them. Brynn was there—he was the one who'd knocked Jack over—along with a couple other guys she'd seen before.

"I think all those guys are in the Latin Society."

"Yup. I was in Latin Society as well."

"Really?" That explained why Jack knew so much about it. "Why'd you leave?"

At first Jack didn't say anything. "It just wasn't for me." He walked quickly up the stairs, Cadel following behind him. Emmy wanted to ask more questions, but she really didn't know Jack that well. She didn't want to seem nosy. But she couldn't help but wonder what made Jack leave Latin Society, and why he couldn't tell her about it.

CHAPTER 6

The Assignment

"Ugh, why do we have to walk all the way to the bloody library for humanities class today?" Lola asked.

Jack took a deep breath, and Emmy smothered a smile. Lola had been grumbling ever since they left the fine arts building, and it was definitely grating on Jack's nerves.

"How is it that you'll run for two hours straight at football practice, but you can't walk an extra ten minutes without going on about it?" Jack asked.

"That's just it," Lola said as they trudged up another flight of stairs. "I ran for two hours last night, and now I'm tired."

Jack shook his head and stuffed his earbuds into his ears.

"Have you played football for a long time?" Emmy asked.

Lola nodded. "I think my dad bought me a football while my mum was in labor. We go to matches every time I make it back to Glasgow."

Emmy smiled, but she didn't feel happy. She'd never know if her dad was a soccer fan.

"Do you play any sports?" Lola asked.

Emmy's heart skipped a beat. "Uh, I used to." She didn't want to explain why her mom wouldn't let her play. She didn't understand it herself.

"I could never give it up," Lola said. "Staring down a keeper, figuring where they'll move next, hearing the crowd cheer—it just becomes part of you, know what I mean?"

Emmy did know what she meant. It made her chest ache to think about it.

"Plus, I get to bash people about without getting in trouble, which is great." Lola winked, and Emmy laughed. Lola seemed like she'd be really fun to play with.

They walked past the giant oak doors that led to the Hall and through the narrow passageway that hitched the strange library tower onto the main building. They threw their bags down and sat at the nearest table just as Master Barlowe walked in. He crouched down beside the table and smiled at Emmy.

"I wanted to check in with you before class started. How are you getting on at Wellsworth so far?"

"Okay, I guess."

"I hear you joined the Latin Society. If you don't mind my saying so, I think your time might be better spent in one of the humanities disciplines, like the Anglo-Saxon or Shakespeare Societies. Shall I speak to Master Larraby about transferring you?"

"Oh, uh…" Emmy wasn't a fan of Latin Society, but at least it gave her a quiet place to catch up on work. She didn't really want to give that up. "Madam Boyd really wanted me in Latin Society, so I think I'd better stick with it."

Barlowe smiled, but he looked a little disappointed. "All right, well, let me know if you change your mind. Latin Society isn't for everyone." He turned away, and Emmy frowned. That was two teachers who had tried to convince her to leave Latin Society.

"All right, let's get started," Barlowe said to the class. "I'm sure you're all wondering why we're meeting in the library today."

Lola muttered something inaudible, and Emmy shook her head. Lola definitely had a hard time keeping her feelings to herself.

"We've been talking about the Dissolution of the Monasteries," Barlowe said. "I trust by now you all know what a critical part it played in British history. Who can tell me one of the reasons why the dissolution was so important?"

The room was quiet. Finally, Natalie raised her hand. "The king made himself the head of the Church of England?"

"Correct," Barlowe said. "That meant he could take all the church's property, assets, and artifacts for himself. Many clergy who resisted were executed, and many priceless artifacts were lost or destroyed.

"And that brings us to our assignment," he went on. "You will get into groups of two or three and research a building that was affected by the Dissolution of the Monasteries. Did the clergy resist? What kinds of artifacts did the building hold? What happened to them? What has happened to that building since? Extra credit will be given to those who put in extra effort, so this isn't a good assignment to skive off on."

Everyone started gathering into groups, and Emmy bit her lip. Being the new kid usually meant being the last to get picked.

"So, where do we start?" Jack asked.

Emmy held her breath. Was Jack just talking to Lola, or did he want Emmy to join them?

"The architectural section, obviously," Lola said. She grabbed her bag and started marching toward one of the long spiral staircases that led to the upper floors. Jack trailed behind her, but Emmy hung back.

Lola started clattering up the staircase and looked over her shoulder. "Aren't you coming, Emmy?"

Emmy smiled and grabbed her bag. She raced up the iron stairs. "Does your library really have an architecture section?"

"Of course," Lola said. "Didn't yours?"

Emmy laughed. "The last school I went to barely even had a library. We just looked everything up online."

"I bet that's what most people are doing," Jack whispered to Emmy, "and they'll probably be done before we've even chosen our building."

Lola stomped up the stairs. "I heard that!" She led them through the maze of stacks and shelves. The library was massive. Its strange octagon shape made it nearly impossible to navigate, but Lola seemed to know it like the back of her hand. Finally, she stopped in the middle of a row. "Here, medieval architecture."

"How do you know where everything is in here?" Emmy asked.

Lola scowled, but didn't say anything.

"After she slugged Brynn in first year she had to do a little 'community service,'" Jack said.

"I spent three months restocking shelves," Lola muttered. "I don't see why Brynn should've complained. His nose looks much better since I broke it."

"Why don't you guys get along?" Emmy asked.

"Because he's a prat," Lola said. "He thinks his side of the family is so much better than ours because they have more money."

Emmy blinked. She knew there were people who thought having money made you better than other people. After all, she'd gone to elite private schools all over New England, and she'd seen plenty of snobs. But it was jarring to hear Lola say it so matter-of-factly.

Lola pulled an enormous book off the shelf and heaved it onto a nearby table. "*Gothic Architecture in Britain*—there ought to be something in here." She flipped the book open and started running her finger over the index. "Westminster Abbey, Canterbury Cathedral, York Minster... I don't know, they're all the same to me."

Emmy sat down in a nearby window seat. "We need something unique, something no one else is doing. I need those extra effort points." She tapped her fingers against the heavy window pane. The stone passageway was right underneath her, making a bridge to the old Hall, which had stood for so many centuries, with its aging stonework and crumbling statuaries. The Hall… So many centuries…

She jumped out of her seat. "The Hall!"

"What about it?" Jack asked.

"We should do the Hall! It used to be a cathedral, right? I bet it was here before the Dissolution of the Monasteries."

"I remember reading that it used to be called Blacehol Abbey," Lola said. "Let's see if we can find it in one of these books."

They searched the shelves, pulling off every book they thought might be relevant. After half an hour, Emmy slumped down in her chair and leaned her head against her hand. "Has anyone found anything?"

"Nope," Lola said. "Seems like there's something about every church in the country except this one."

"Maybe it just wasn't important enough to make it into any books," Jack said.

Lola shook her head. "But that doesn't make sense. Abbeys were always important. We read about them last year, remember?"

"Not everyone remembers every page of every book they've ever read, Lola."

"So, what are we going to do?" Emmy asked. "Should we just pick something else?"

"I think the mezzanine has a section with local history books," Lola said. "It's a bit of a long shot, but we could try."

The mezzanine was at the top of a set of rickety steps, and it felt more like an attic than a library. Emmy wrinkled her nose. The air stunk of moldy leather and some kind of toxic dung. "Are there bats up here?"

Lola ignored her and walked to the far side of the loft. "This is the local history section, but I haven't got a clue if we'll find anything. Most of these books are so old they don't even have titles on the covers."

Emmy ran her fingers along the dusty leather spines. "If they don't even have titles, how are we supposed to..." She stopped. One of the books had a strange symbol, a symbol she had seen before: a skull with a cross on the right and a dagger on the left.

"I've seen this symbol before." She pulled the book off the shelf. "It's on a stone outside the Latin Society."

Jack took the book from Emmy and looked at the spine. "Oh, that just means the book will be in Latin." He put it back on the shelf. "I don't think there's anything up here, we should just choose another church."

"I've never seen that symbol before, and I've been taking Latin for years." Lola said. "Is that a skull?"

"Yeah, I think so." Emmy grabbed the book and opened the cracked leather cover. "It's not in Latin, and it's called *Wellsworth School for Boys: An Early History*. This is exactly what we need!" She looked at Jack. "Why did you think it would be in Latin?"

He chewed his bottom lip. "I guess I got the symbol mixed up with something else."

Emmy flipped the pages until she found a table of contents. "Looks like there are three whole chapters about Blacehol Abbey. That should be enough for our report."

"I could read them," Jack said, "and tell you guys what they say."

"No, that's okay," Emmy said, "we can each take a chapter."

"Seriously, I don't mind, I'll just—"

"What's gotten into you?" Lola asked. "Since when do you want to do extra reading?"

Jack shrugged his shoulders. "I just want to help."

"We're supposed to do equal work on group projects," Emmy said.

"But how are we all supposed to read the book at the same time?"

"Why don't we just photocopy the first three chapters and we can each take one."

"And then leave the book here?" Jack said.

Emmy nodded.

"Okay, but just the first three chapters, right?"

"What does it matter if—"

"I just don't think we need to do extra reading. We're supposed to learn about the Abbey, not the school."

Lola rolled her eyes. "It takes, what, ten minutes to read a chapter?"

"No, it takes *you* ten minutes to read a chapter." Jack glared at Lola. "Not all of us are speed readers with photographic memories."

Emmy left them sniping at each other, got the chapters copied, and gave the book to the librarian. Then, she handed Jack and Lola a chapter each. "We can read them tonight during study session and talk about them after."

As soon as study session ended, they all got together at a table near the fire.

"I can't understand why there aren't more books about Blacehol Abbey." Lola glanced at Madam Boyd's door and popped a stick of gum in her mouth. "My chapter says it was part of Blacehol Monastery, which was a really important place in the Middle Ages. It had one of the biggest art collections in Britain. Their monks were expert metalworkers, and they made amazing things out of silver and pewter."

"My chapter talks about the monastery, too," Emmy said. "Apparently the monks put up a huge fight when the monastery was dissolved. Eventually they were all executed for treason, but they managed to hide their entire art collection first."

"Really?" Lola said. "Where did they hide it?"

"Beats me," Emmy said.

Lola looked at Jack. "So, what's your chapter about?"

Jack tapped his fingers on the table. "Mostly the same stuff as yours. Then it starts talking about the school, and there's not much useful there."

Emmy stared at Jack. "Um, really? 'Cause I read it, too, and I thought there was lots of stuff we could use."

"What are you talking about?" Lola asked.

"I flipped through his chapter when I was photocopying it, and it looked really interesting, so I copied it for myself, too."

Jack stopped tapping. "You read my chapter? I can't believe you—"

"So, what'd you dig up?" Lola interrupted.

"It's about the school's founding, and it's got a lot of cool stuff. Listen to this." Emmy began to read. "Of all the contributions our school has made to British society, none is greater than our noble brotherhood: the Order of Black Hollow Lane."

CHAPTER 7

The Order of Black Hollow Lane

"What's the Order of Black Hollow Lane?" Lola asked.

Jack cleared his throat. "I don't think we should—"

"I think it's some kind of secret society," Emmy interrupted.

Lola dropped her notebook on the table. "A secret society? At Wellsworth?"

"Yeah," Emmy said, "at least they were here when the school first started. And that weird skull thing is the symbol for the Order. They put it on things to let other Order members know when something was important. Almost like a secret handshake, but one you can actually see and leave behind."

"That is so cool!" Lola said.

"I know! They sound kind of creepy, though. Apparently, they—"

"Let's go for a walk!" Jack shoved his chair back so hard it tipped over.

"A walk?" Emmy looked at her watch. It was after eight thirty, and they weren't allowed out past nine.

"Yeah, it'll do us good after being cooped up in here all evening."

"Have you gone mental?" Lola said. "It's pitch black and freezing outside."

"I just need some fresh air."

Emmy looked at Lola and shrugged, but they both followed Jack.

The icy wind blasted them the minute Jack opened the door. Emmy hugged her sweater tight to her body.

"There," Jack said through chattering teeth. "That's loads better."

Lola shook her head. "Mental. So what else did you find out, Emmy?"

"This Order was pretty creepy. They thought they needed

to 'purge the school of dissenting viewpoints,' which I think means getting rid of anyone who doesn't agree with them. And they had this ritual where new recruits would cut their hands open and let the blood drip down onto a human skull."

Lola stuck out her tongue. "Blech!"

"I know, and they had to say this pledge where they promised that 'nothing and no one' was more important than the Order. It's like something out of a scary movie. I don't know what Black Hollow Lane is, though. It's kind of a weird name."

"It probably comes from Blacehol Abbey," Lola said. "*Blace* means black in Old English, and *Hol* means hollow."

"How do you know that?"

"We did a bit of Anglo-Saxon language study in humanities last year."

Emmy raised her eyebrows. "And you remember what random words mean?"

"I told you," Jack said, "she remembers every page of every book she's ever read."

"Anyways, the Anglo-Saxons often named places after things that were nearby," Lola said. "There might have actually been some kind of lane in a black hollow at some point."

Emmy nodded. "So, do you think we should put something about them in our report?"

"No." Jack rubbed the goose bumps on his arms. "I think we should just forget about them."

"But this could really make our report stand out!" Emmy said.

"You don't understand how dangerous they are!"

Lola crossed her arms and narrowed her eyes. "All right, Jack. Spill it."

Jack kicked at the icy dirt. "I don't know what you're—"

"Come on, you obviously know something about this Order thing," Lola said. "You'd better give us a good reason if you want us to keep quiet about them."

Jack looked around the empty clearing. "I don't know a lot," he said quietly. "I just know they exist…and that they're dangerous."

"How do you know about them?" Emmy asked.

"My dad's a member, and Malcolm and Vincent. Brynn's a member, too. That's why he hates me."

"Why would being part of the Order make Brynn hate you?"

Jack stuffed his hands inside his pockets. "Most people don't find out about the Order until they're in the last year or two at school. It was different for Brynn and me. Our families have a long history in the Order, so we were offered a…well, I guess you'd call it an apprenticeship. We were supposed to start early training so that when we left school, we'd have some kind of special positions or something. Brynn was really excited about us doing all this stuff together."

"So, what happened?" Emmy asked.

"Vincent was supposed to be in charge of our first year's training. That's when he was still at school. He offered me the apprenticeship…and I said no."

"You turned your brother down?"

Jack nodded.

"Why?"

Jack leaned against the door. "Malcolm and Vincent…they changed when they joined the Order. I don't know what they all have to do, but I know some of it isn't legal. And a lot of it seems pretty dangerous, and it puts other people in danger, too. So, I told Vincent I didn't want to do it, pulled out of Latin Society, and that was that."

"What does Latin Society have to do with the Order?" Emmy asked.

"It's like a recruitment ground, a place to find worthy candidates," Jack explained. "They test people with questions and challenges to find out if they've got what it takes. If they pass the tests, they're offered the chance to join before they leave school."

"They haven't asked me any questions," Emmy said.

Jack laughed. "The Order might as well hang up a big 'No Girls Allowed' sign. And believe me, if the Order is ignoring you, that's a good thing."

"Are you… I mean…" Emmy didn't know how to say this. "Are you safe at home?"

"Oh yeah, it's nothing like that," Jack said quickly. "I don't get on with my family, but they don't scare me. I just hear things sometimes, things that Malcolm or Vincent are doing that sound kind of shady. I know those things are for the Order."

"How come I didn't know all this?" Lola had been strangely quiet while Jack was talking. Her face was bright red, and Emmy couldn't tell if she was angry or hurt. Maybe it was a bit of both.

"Most of it happened before we started hanging out. My dad's still on me about joining the Order, though."

Emmy bit her fingernail. "I guess we probably shouldn't talk about them in our humanities report."

"Definitely not. I'd be in loads of trouble if anyone found out what I told you."

"Don't worry," Emmy said, "your secret's safe with us. And there's plenty of information on the abbey in that book. We'll just focus on that for the report."

Jack let out a big breath. They went back inside and kept working on the assignment, but Emmy's mind kept wandering back to Jack and the Order. He hadn't known her that long, but he told her something really personal and kind of scary. She hadn't even told Jack and Lola about her dad. It was just so hard to explain that her dad was a total mystery to her. She didn't even know what had happened to him. What if they didn't understand? What if they thought it was weird? What if they thought *she* was weird? She'd never really had close friends before. She couldn't do anything that might mess that up.

"Emmy, did you hear what I said?" Lola was staring at her.

"Oh, sorry, what was that?"

"Where was that stuff about the monks being executed for treason?"

"I'll find it." Emmy riffled through her pages. She needed to focus—she didn't want to let Jack and Lola down.

It took them a few days to finish the assignment. Emmy smiled when she handed it in to Master Barlowe. She was proud of this report; they'd worked really hard on it.

"Blacehol Abbey?" Barlowe looked at her. "I'm surprised you found information on our old cathedral. It can be hard to come by."

"We found an old book in the library mezzanine. There was lots of stuff about the abbey and about when the school was founded."

Barlowe tapped their report on his desk a few times. "You must have found some interesting information in there."

"Yeah, lots, but we didn't have time to go through it all. We just focused on the abbey for the report."

"Good," he said sharply. "That was the goal of the assignment. Sometimes doing extra work isn't a good thing. Do you still have the book?"

Emmy shook her head.

"Good."

Emmy tucked her hair behind her ear. Barlowe didn't seem too impressed by the extra effort they'd put in. He seemed almost annoyed. She let the next person hand in his report and went back to her seat. They didn't need anything else for their assignment, but she couldn't help but be curious about the Order. Who wouldn't want to know more about an ancient secret society? It felt a bit strange to go to Latin Society now that she knew they had a connection to this weird group, but it's not like they had any interest in her. She'd probably never hear anything about the Order again.

CHAPTER 8

The Saint

The next few weeks were a blur. Get up, go to class, study. Eat lunch, go to class, study. It was exhausting. Researching her father's box seemed like a lost cause. Every once in a while, she'd stare at the medallions or try and fit them together like a puzzle, but it never worked. That was as much research as she had time for now that school had become her whole life.

She kept going to Latin Society, even though nobody helped her with Latin. In fact, nobody talked to her at all. Other people had joined since she started, and most of them already seemed like "part of the club." Malcolm and Brynn made a point of chatting with almost every new boy, asking them questions, and helping them fit in.

Malcolm seemed to have a special status in the club. Everybody wanted to sit with him, like he was some kind of good luck charm. He was so different from Jack: outgoing, loud, always the center of attention. He was friendly with everybody in the club—everybody except Emmy. She wondered whether he knew she was friends with his brother and if that made a difference.

On top of all that, her mom was sending almost daily messages badgering Emmy to work harder. Like that was even possible. She'd never worked so hard in her life. The worst part was, her mom hadn't once mentioned her birthday. Birthdays had always been awkward. Emmy's dad had left on her third birthday, and her mom wanted to forget everything about that day. But turning twelve was a big deal. Wasn't it?

The morning of her birthday, Emmy met Lola in the common room.

"So, today's the big day!" Lola said with a grin.

Emmy's cheeks felt flushed. "How did you find out?"

"In first year, like everyone else."

Emmy looked blankly at Lola. "Wait, what are you talking about?"

"It's Saint Audrey's Feast Day! We get a proper feast tonight to honor our house's illustrious patron, Saint Audrey."

"Audrey was a saint?" Emmy asked.

"Sure, all the houses are named after saints," Jack said as he sauntered down the Edmund staircase. "Edmund, Felix, Withburga...they were all saints from this part of England."

Emmy nodded. She'd wondered where the name Withburga had come from.

"Come on, I'm starving," Lola said.

They hurried to the Hall and filled their plates with food. They had just sat down when someone cleared his throat behind them. "Morning, Jack."

Jack didn't turn around. "Hey, Malcolm." He stared straight down and kept poking at the sausages on his plate.

"This is from Dad." Malcolm handed Jack an envelope. "He asked me to give it to you when I went home last weekend."

Jack looked up for the first time. "You went home for the weekend?"

Emmy bit her lip. Why hadn't Jack been invited? The look on his face made her think Jack was wondering the same thing.

"I had some business to take care of...for Dad."

Jack's face went tight, like he was trying not to wince. "Right. Was that what you were doing when you and Dev fell off the chapter house?"

Malcolm looked around and crouched down beside Jack. "Look, I didn't want him to come with me, okay? And it wasn't 'business.' You think I'd let some kid come with me on business?"

"Then what was he doing with you?"

"I told you, it wasn't my idea. Somebody dared me to walk along the edge, and... I don't know, somehow he just ended up coming with me. He got freaked out and lost his balance. I grabbed him and pushed him back onto the wider part of the roof, but then I fell."

Jack looked down at his plate of sausages. "That's it?"

"That's it. That's the whole story." Malcolm stared straight at his brother, like he was ready for a challenge.

"Fine," Jack said.

Malcolm stood up and walked away. Emmy didn't know what to make of him or his awkward relationship with Jack.

Classes went by slowly that day. She kept checking her phone for missed calls from her mom, but there was nothing. She just wanted to crawl into bed and wait for her birthday to be over.

After the long walk back from Latin Society, Emmy trudged up the Audrey stairs, opened the door to her room, and just about threw up.

The smell was overwhelming. Victoria was sitting on Emmy's bed with four different nail polish bottles open on her nightstand. Her friend Arabella was sitting beside her, the dust from her nail file sprinkling over Emmy's bedspread.

"Can't you do that somewhere else?" Emmy said as she pulled her shirt up over her nose.

Victoria smiled sweetly. "Nope." She carefully placed an open nail polish on Emmy's pillow.

Emmy stared at the open bottle and shook her head. She'd had it with Victoria. "Get that stuff off my pillow."

Victoria teetered toward Emmy, her freshly polished toes curled up and away from the fuzzy carpet. "Make me." Her face was two inches away from Emmy's, and she stared straight into Emmy's eyes.

Emmy stared straight back.

Do it, she thought.

She clenched her fists.

Just this once.

She moved a little closer to Victoria. They were nose to nose.

"Get it off my bed." Emmy gritted her teeth. "Now."

Victoria swallowed hard and glanced at Arabella, who was sitting stock still. Emmy smirked. They hadn't expected her to stand her ground.

"Fine," Victoria said, her voice cracking a little. She nodded to Arabella, who picked up the nail polish, put on the cap, and tossed it and the nail file onto Victoria's bed.

Emmy took a deep breath and picked up her economics textbook. Maybe she could get a few more chapters read before dinner. She turned toward the door, but the heavy book slipped out of her fingers…and landed right on Victoria's toes.

Victoria shrieked and grabbed her foot, hopping and lunging toward Emmy. She flew forward and landed face-first on the floor. Emmy giggled and Victoria lunged from her hands and knees, her feet dragging on the fluffy white carpet.

"Your toes!" Arabella screeched.

A trail of pink goo streaked across the floor. Victoria screamed and flipped onto her back, legs flailing like a cockroach that couldn't find its feet.

"It took me an hour to get my toes just right! You did that on purpose, you little witch!"

"I didn't even do anything!"

"Oh, really? Was that an accident?" Victoria sat up and

grabbed the nail polish off her bed. "Then I'm going to cause a little *accident*, too!" She swiped Emmy's economics textbook, wrenched open the bottle, and slowly tipped it upside down.

"No!" Emmy yelled, but it was too late. Nail polish was dribbling down into the textbook, oozing between the pages.

"Oops!" Victoria flipped through the book, making sure each page got a generous dollop of sticky pink polish. "Had a little spill! And if you don't want me to have an 'accident' with any of your other books, I'd suggest you get out of MY room!"

Emmy pressed her lips together, then felt her shoulders slump. *It's not worth it. Just go. Let her win. Again.* She reached for the door handle and walked out.

"Bye-bye!" A chorus of giggles rang out, and Emmy started to run. She ran down the stairs and flew out the door, knocking over a couple of first years as she went. She ran and ran, following the trail farther into the forest.

The pines grew thicker here. Their heavy branches bowed into the trail, slapping at Emmy with sharp blue needles. She kept running. The smell of the pines started mingling with something else, something she hadn't noticed before—salt.

Was Wellsworth near the ocean?

The smell got stronger the farther she ran. The ground felt

soft and squishy, with patches of mud here and there. The trees were getting thinner, and soon she reached the forest's edge.

She'd never seen anything like it. A wide valley of mud stretched out in front of her with two towering cliffs on either side. Layers of red rock were woven together with long bands of bright white that stretched across the cliff face.

"What's that white stuff?" she muttered to herself.

"Chalk."

Emmy jumped. Jonas, the man who had picked her up from the airport, was standing a few feet away. He was wearing thigh-high rubber boots and carrying a bucket with a rake resting on his shoulder.

"That white rock inside the cliffs, it's chalk. Makes for quite a pretty view, even though it'll all tumble down into the North Sea eventually."

"It will?"

"Sure. Every day the sea floods this valley, and when the tide goes back out it takes a little more rock with it. One day the sea will steal all of North Norfolk."

"Really?" Emmy asked.

Jonas chuckled. "In a few thousand years, give or take. So, what brings you out here, young miss?"

Emmy looked down and shrugged. She didn't want to talk

about Victoria, or school, or her birthday. She didn't want to say that her mother had forgotten it. Again. Or that she had to spend it without a father. Again.

Jonas put down his bucket and started pulling his rake through the sand. After a few tries his rake pulled up a clam, which he picked up and threw in the bucket. "Something got you riled up?"

Emmy shrugged again.

Jonas dropped another clam in his bucket. "You know, I had a bit of a tough time adjusting when I was in my first year. Most people were okay, but there were a few who were just impossible to get on with. I was lucky, though. I had a great roommate. Made all the difference."

Emmy blinked back tears. "Mine is horrible. I don't know how I'm going to live with her for the rest of the year. Maybe... maybe I should go home."

"Maybe," Jonas said.

Emmy looked up. She hadn't really expected him to agree with her.

"I guess it all comes down to what got you on that plane in the first place," Jonas said. "It's like I said on your first day. You're the only one who knows if it's worth it."

Emmy tucked her hair behind her ear. Her father's box

was still sitting under her bed, right where she had put it on her first day. She'd been so busy, she'd barely had time to think about it, let alone get it out. Besides, if Victoria found out about it, she'd probably trash it, just like her economics textbook.

"I don't want to give up," Emmy said, "but I don't know what to do next."

Plop. Another clam went into the bucket.

"I couldn't help but notice you usually sit with the same two people at lunch. One of the Galt boys and Madam Boyd's daughter, am I right?"

Emmy shook her head. "I don't sit with Madam Boyd's daughter."

"Sure, you do. Black hair, from Glasgow—can't remember her name."

Emmy stared at Jonas. "Lola?"

"Lola, that's it," Jonas said. "Lola Boyd."

Emmy couldn't believe it. Lola was Madam Boyd's daughter? How could she not have known that?

Jonas threw another clam in the bucket. "Can't be that easy having your mother as your head of house. And the Galt boy—it's John, isn't it?"

"Jack," Emmy said.

"That's right, Jack. I don't think he's had the easiest time of it, either. Might be worth having a chat with them."

Emmy looked at the ground. She didn't usually confide in people.

"It's hard to find people you can trust," Jonas said. He threw another clam in the bucket. "Give them a chance, and give Wellsworth a chance, too. I think you'll be surprised. I bet by the end of the year, Wellsworth will be in your blood, just like it's in mine."

Emmy looked away. There were some things she liked about Wellsworth. She liked Jack and Lola, that was for sure. But the school itself? She didn't feel much of a connection to it. She'd never really felt connected anywhere. It seemed pretty unlikely that a place could ever be "in her blood."

Jonas flung his rake in a new direction. "And when it comes to that roommate… Well, in my experience bullies don't usually bother pushing people who push back."

Jack and Lola were sitting in the common room when Emmy got back. They were playing a card game Lola had invented that involved a lot of slapping of piles and shoving the other person out of the way.

"You're not Madam Boyd's daughter, are you?" Emmy asked.

Lola snatched a stack of cards from Jack's side of the table. "Took you this long to figure that out, did it? Same last name, same accent, same winning personality." She slapped her hand on a card and added it to one of her stacks.

Jack laid out four more cards and just managed to get his hand on one before Lola grabbed it.

"Is it weird having your mom as your head of house?"

Lola shrugged. "It's not so bad. I don't really know any different."

Emmy chewed on her lower lip. There was something she'd been wondering about for a while, but she hadn't figured out if it was okay to ask. "Your mom doesn't seem very old. Why does she walk with a cane?"

"She was in an accident," Lola said. "Tore the inside of her knee to shreds."

There was a flurry of cards and both Jack and Lola emptied their stacks onto new ones. Jack pulled at his hair and groaned.

"Gotcha!" Lola grinned and turned to Emmy. "What about your mum? She writes books telling people all the things they're doing wrong with their kids, right?"

Emmy laughed. "Something like that."

"Do you hear from her much?" Jack asked.

"Yeah, but not today." Emmy sighed. "I think she forgot that today's my birthday."

"It's your birthday?" Lola said. "Why didn't you tell us!?"

Emmy shrugged. "I'm not really a birthday person."

"What about your dad?" Jack asked. "Did he send you anything?"

"Um, no."

Jack and Lola looked at her like they expected her to say more. She tucked her hair behind her ear. She didn't *have* to say anything else. But Jonas's words kept coming back to her. *Give them a chance.*

She took a deep breath. "My dad disappeared on my third birthday. The police said it was really suspicious, and that someone probably..." Emmy swallowed, "...did something to him, but no one really knows for sure."

"But then..." Jack hesitated. "Then he could have just...left?"

Emmy didn't say anything. *This* was why she hadn't talked about her dad before. Because she didn't want to answer that question. Finally, she nodded. "Maybe."

The table went quiet. Lola tapped her cards, and Jack kept running his fingers through his hair.

"Look," Lola said, "I know it's not the same, but I know what it's like to miss my dad. And Jack, well," she glanced at Jack and he looked down at the table, "he's never really known his dad at all. Not really."

Jack nodded, but he didn't look up.

"I guess all I'm trying to say is…you're not alone here."

Emmy pressed her eyes tight to keep any tears from falling. She'd never been any place where she didn't feel alone. Maybe she'd finally found one.

Lola cleared her throat. "All right, enough sappiness, it's making us all dreary and you can't have a lousy birthday this year. Saint Audrey wouldn't approve. Come on, let's go to the feast."

They stood up and were walking to the door when Victoria walked past and bumped extra hard into Emmy. She snickered and Emmy sighed.

"I'm so sick of her."

Lola shook her head. "You've got to stop letting her push you around."

"I tried."

"So, try again," Lola said. "Show her you're not just some wishy-washy little girl."

"But how?"

Lola flashed a smile. "Some people might punch her, but I frown on that sort of thing."

Emmy laughed and felt a warm rush in her chest. She'd always wanted a friend who made her laugh like Lola did.

Emmy followed them out the door, then stopped. Punching Victoria wasn't exactly her style, but maybe there was something else she could do.

She bit her lip and smiled.

"Are you coming?" Jack asked. "You can't miss out on the chance to eat an Audrey feast while the rest of us are stuck with plain old Hall food."

"Uh, I'll catch up. There's something I need to do first."

She dashed up the stairs and grabbed a pencil and pen from her backpack. Her economics textbook had been tossed on her bed, but thankfully the nail polish hadn't dribbled onto her bedspread. Emmy ignored her own book and rummaged through Victoria's textbooks until she found the one she was looking for: a pristine, barely opened copy of *Economics for Third Form*. She opened the cover and carefully erased Victoria's name, then wrote in a new one in pen. She grabbed the nail polish–soaked book, put it on Victoria's bed, and grinned as she wrote her roommate a note.

Emmy dug into the feast with gusto, but after trying a pie that seemed to be filled with cold slabs of pork sitting in Jell-O, she was a little more cautious. The Audrey girls brought leftovers to the common room and were sharing them with the Edmund boys when a piercing scream rang out from upstairs. A bunch of people ran to the stairs to see what was going on, but Emmy ignored them and popped a piece of marzipan-covered cake into her mouth.

Victoria flew down the staircase and stomped over to Emmy. "What is this supposed to mean?" She waved a piece of paper in Emmy's face.

Emmy cocked her head to one side. "Just what it says. I borrowed your economics textbook this morning."

"What do you mean, you borrowed my economics textbook?" Victoria screeched.

"Well, I couldn't find mine, so I borrowed yours. I was coming back to return it when I accidentally dropped it on your toes. Sorry about that, by the way."

Victoria held up the polish-soaked textbook. "This is YOUR book, not mine!"

"It can't be, I have mine right here." Emmy held up a crisp, clean economics textbook and pointed to the inside cover. "See? It has my name in it."

Victoria tried to open the front cover of her book, but the first few pages were completely stuck together.

"That sure was a nasty spill," Emmy said sweetly. "You ought to be more careful."

Victoria clenched her jaw. "You switched these books, I know you did!"

"I don't know what you're talking about. But you're welcome to take your suspicions to Madam Boyd. I'm sure she'd love to hear all about how that little spill happened." She smiled and put another slice of cake on her plate.

Victoria stood there for a few moments before storming off, taking the ruined book with her.

Jack and Lola stared at Emmy.

"Is that really your book?" Jack asked.

"Of course not," Emmy whispered. "She dumped nail polish in mine, so I switched them before dinner. Not like it was hard—I just erased her name and wrote mine in. That's why you should always use pen."

Lola shook her head. "Not bad for your first act of vengeance."

Emmy's phone dinged. She pulled it out of her pocket, read the new text message, and sighed.

"What's up?" Jack asked.

"From my mom," Emmy said, and she read the text aloud. "'Sorry I couldn't call, Em, I was filming all day and I'm just about to get on a plane to Denver. I transferred some money into your account as a birthday present. Next year I'll do something more special, I promise! Love you.'"

Lola grinned. "Cash in your bank account's not bad, is it?"

"Yeah, I guess." Cash was nice, but a phone call would have been nicer.

CHAPTER 9

Christmas

The closer it got to Christmas, the less people seemed to be paying attention to their schoolwork. Working in the common room was hopeless, but Emmy didn't mind. She was one of only a handful of students who wasn't going home for the holidays, and with Victoria gone, she could use the break to catch up on schoolwork. In the meantime, she was happy to hang out in the common room, listen to punk rock carols, and snap the little gift packages called Christmas crackers with whichever third year had gotten their hands on some that day. Emmy didn't miss being in Connecticut at all. Her mom usually spent the holidays working on her latest book, and being with friends at Wellsworth was a lot merrier than sitting in an empty living room and staring at an artificial tree.

The school got a lot quieter on the last day before Christmas break. Lola left at lunchtime to catch a train to Glasgow to see her dad, and by the time Emmy finished her last class, it seemed like half the school was gone. She walked Jack out to the parking lot while he waited for his ride home.

Malcolm was there, too, but he stood on the opposite end of the lot, playing on his phone like his brother wasn't even there.

"Who's picking you up?" Emmy asked.

"Vincent, I think."

"Is that your oldest brother? The one who left school a couple years ago?"

Jack nodded. "He works for my dad now." He picked up his suitcase. "There's his car."

A silver sports car pulled into the drive and stopped right beside Malcolm. The driver jumped out, pulled Malcolm into a tight side hug and slapped him on the back.

"I'd better go," Jack said. "Happy Christmas, Emmy."

"Merry Christmas."

Jack pulled his suitcase across the parking lot and threw it into the trunk. He hopped in the back seat, and it didn't look like he or his brothers even said hello.

Emmy wandered back to the mostly empty common room and got out her schoolbooks. She worked most of the day and the next day, too. By Christmas Eve, she had made a serious dent in all the reading and worksheets that had been looming over her since she arrived.

Emmy woke up early on Christmas morning. Master Barlowe had arranged for a bus to take people into the nearby town of King's Lynn for the day. Apparently, they were going to a concert, which didn't sound that interesting, but it was better than doing homework on Christmas day.

It didn't take long for the bus to get to King's Lynn. Emmy had never seen so much brick in her life. Some were rusty red, some dingy gray, and some in a black-and-white checkered pattern that seemed like it had been there forever. Finally, the bus stopped in front of an old stone church.

"Here are your tickets," Master Barlowe said as he walked up the aisle. "Make sure you're back on board by two o'clock."

Emmy grabbed her ticket and had just hopped off the bus when her phone rang. "Hello?"

"Merry Christmas, darling!" her mother sang.

"Merry Christmas, Mom."

"How was your morning?"

"Pretty good, actually. We had a huge English breakfast this morning, and we're just about to go to a concert."

"That sounds lovely. I'm in New Mexico. We're taking a break from filming over the holidays, but it didn't seem worth it to go all the way back to Connecticut when there wasn't anyone there."

Other students jostled past Emmy and went into the church. She checked her watch; she had a few minutes yet. "How's filming going?"

"All right, I guess. I don't really get to see much other than the hotel and the house of whichever family I'm working with."

Emmy wrinkled her nose. That didn't sound like much fun. "Are you meeting lots of people?"

"Constantly," her mom said. "There are producers and more crew than I ever imagined, and I don't actually spend that much time with the families. Most of it is just filming whatever some producer or director tells us to do that day. It's strange. There are people everywhere all the time, but it's actually kind of lonely."

The phone got quiet. Emmy didn't know what to say. It

didn't really sound like her mother was all that happy, but what could Emmy do about that?

"But the work is the important part," her mom said. "It's all about helping people. I'm sure it must be helping someone."

"Yeah, I'm sure it is." She checked her watch. "Sorry, Mom. I have to go, the concert's about to start."

"All right, have fun. I wish I could be there with you!" Her voice cracked.

Emmy bit her lip. "Merry Christmas, Mom."

"Merry Christmas, darling."

Emmy hung up and raced across the parking lot. A priest stood outside the arched door and smiled at her.

"May I see your ticket?"

Emmy handed it to him.

"Ah, ticket number twenty-three," he murmured. His eyes lingered on Emmy, as if he had seen her before and was trying to figure out when. He smiled, but it seemed more sad than happy. "Here's a program. Please, let me check your coat."

Emmy took the brochure and handed him her coat.

"You'd better go in, the concert's about to begin."

Emmy slipped inside the door and let it close gently behind her. The room was packed but silent. If she could spy an empty seat, she might be able to snag it before the music started. Then a voice broke the silence. High. Clear. Magnified by some ancient magic that still breathed in the old stone walls. There was an empty seat at the end of a nearby bench, but Emmy didn't move. Her footsteps might break the spell.

Then one voice broke into two, and then three, and then a chorus of voices weaved in and out of each other like threads being pulled into a tapestry. Emmy closed her eyes and leaned into a pillar.

Lully, lullay, thou little tiny child.

It was a lullaby. And it was the saddest lullaby she'd ever heard.

Bye, bye, lully, lullay. This poor youngling for whom we sing, bye, bye, lully, lullay.

Someone was saying goodbye to their child for the last time.

Emmy's chest started to ache. If her dad had said goodbye to her, she didn't remember it. Maybe he'd thought he was coming back. Maybe he didn't know it would be their last goodbye. Or maybe he didn't feel like the parent in this song. Maybe he didn't miss her at all.

A tear dripped down to her chin. It was silly, really. Nobody cried because of a song. The music ended, and she wiped her face clean as she slunk into the nearest bench.

After the concert, Emmy filed out through the doors with

everyone else. The priest handed Emmy her coat and gave her another sad smile. It was strange. Everybody else still had their coats.

She looked back, but the priest had disappeared into the crowd.

Emmy climbed back onto the bus with the handful of other students who had come to the concert. She pulled off her jacket and felt something crinkle in her pocket. It was an envelope. She sat down and opened it.

Inside was a handwritten letter, yellow and crinkled in the corners, as if someone had mailed it years ago and she'd forgotten to throw it away. She squinted at the smudged ink and began to read:

> Dear Tom,
>   The rift between us is a growing concern. Meet me in Hollingworth Square Thursday next at 9:00 p.m.
>   Your Brother Loyola

The bus started moving, and Emmy wrinkled her forehead. This letter wasn't hers. She must have picked it up by mistake and forgotten about it. She was about to stuff it back in her pocket when she noticed there was another paper inside. This one was crisp and new, and only had one sentence:

From the files of Thomas Allyn.

Thomas Allyn. That was her father's name. His *real* name, the one she had seen on the marriage certificate. Emmy chewed on her thumbnail. This couldn't be possible. Letters don't just appear in people's pockets. How was she ending up with so many of her dad's things? Her mom had always kept everything of his away from her. Everything he owned, every trace of him, it was all gone. Except it wasn't. *Somebody* knew. Somebody knew what had happened to him. Somebody had things that belonged to him. And now they were passing them on to her.

Emmy looked at the signature. *Your Brother Loyola.* But her dad didn't have a brother. Did he?

Emmy's heart started beating again. Her mother had always said that her dad had no family. But that didn't really make sense. How could someone have absolutely no family? Her father hadn't been very old when he'd disappeared. How could all of his family be gone?

Emmy read the letter again. *The rift between us.* Her heart beat faster. Could her father have been estranged from his family? Was it possible that members of his family—of her family—were alive and well...and living here in England?

She took a deep breath and closed her eyes. She needed to think. Someone had slipped this letter into her pocket. That person had been at the church, and they had access to her coat. Her eyes flew open.

The priest.

She stuffed the papers back in the envelope and ran into the aisle.

"Emmy?" Master Barlowe put his hand on her shoulder. "We're moving, you'll have to find your seat."

"I need to get off the bus," Emmy said.

Barlowe raised his eyebrows. "Why's that?"

"I need to find somebody, it's urgent!"

"Who do you need to find? Are we missing someone?"

"No, I, uh," Emmy didn't know what to say. "It's someone I met at the concert, it's really important."

"We're on a bit of a tight schedule, Emmy. I'm afraid there isn't time."

The bus turned another corner and Emmy looked back. The two towers of the church faded into the fog and finally disappeared.

CHAPTER 10

Easter Term Begins

Emmy was still thinking about the letter when students started coming back to school a week later. Her holiday had been quiet but peaceful. She spent most evenings curled up by the fire and chatting with Natalie, who was on the soccer team with Lola and hadn't gone home for the holidays, either. It was nice, but Emmy was looking forward to the school getting busier again. It had been overwhelming when she'd first arrived, but now she was used to people spilling out of classrooms and cramming onto couches in the common room. It made the school feel alive. When Jack and Lola showed up, Emmy found herself jumping off the couch and giving them both hugs.

"How were your holidays?" she asked.

Lola scrunched up her face. "Dad's got a new girlfriend, a woman named Lacee who's young enough to be my sister. We asked her to come to a football match, and she said she'd never really understood people who like football."

Emmy cringed. Not liking football was a fast track to Lola's bad side. She looked at Jack. "What about you?"

Jack rubbed a piece of lint off his shirt. "Same as usual. I'm just glad to be back where I belong."

"Me too," Lola said.

Emmy looked at her friends. *Me too*.

"So how was your holiday?" Lola asked.

Emmy bit her lip. She hadn't told anyone about the letter, but she wasn't getting anywhere with trying to figure things out on her own. Maybe it was time to get a little help.

"Come on, I want to show you something."

Emmy led Jack and Lola up the stairs and into her room. Jack hesitated in the doorway. Boys weren't supposed to be on the Audrey side of the building, let alone in the girls' rooms.

"Don't be such a baby," Lola said, "it's not like anyone cares."

Jack came in and quickly shut the door behind him.

Emmy pulled the letter out of her backpack and explained how she'd gotten it. Then she threw herself down on the bed and sighed. "I just don't get it. Why go to all that trouble just to give me an old letter?"

"Well, obviously this person wants you to know that your dad had a brother and that they had some kind of falling-out," Lola said.

"So why not just tell me? And why send me an old letter instead of explaining it in a new one?"

"Maybe there's a reason this person wants to stay anonymous," Jack said. "You're sure you can't think of anyone who could be doing this?"

Emmy tugged at her ear. "I can think of one person…"

"Who?"

"My dad. I think he might be the one doing this. I think he…he might have been that priest. The one at the church."

The room was silent for a few moments. Emmy didn't expect anyone to talk. She didn't know what to say, either.

Suddenly, they heard a girl berating someone outside the door. Victoria was back. Emmy's eyes widened and Lola swore.

"You're not supposed to be in here!" Emmy hissed at Jack. Lola tackled him and shoved him under Victoria's bed just as the door opened.

Emmy smiled at Victoria. That was a mistake.

Victoria eyed them suspiciously. "What are you two up to?"

"Sneaking boys under your bed," Lola said casually.

The room went dead silent. Emmy had to bite her tongue to stop herself from laughing.

"Fine, don't tell me," Victoria said, and she heaved her suitcase on her bed. Jack grunted, and Emmy quickly coughed to cover it up. Victoria's eyes narrowed, and Emmy held her breath.

"You know," Victoria said, "if you're sick, you've got to stay in the medical center. I'm not catching pneumonia because I'm stuck with an unhygienic roommate." She flicked her hair behind her shoulder and left the room. Emmy finally let the air out of her lungs, and Lola started to laugh.

"It's not funny!" Jack crawled out from under the bed and rubbed the back of his head. "First you throw me under the bed, where apparently no one has vacuumed since the Second World War, and then I'm attacked by that bloody bag!"

"Oh, I'm sorry," Lola said, "I didn't realize you'd be overwhelmed by a plastic pink carrying case."

Jack folded his arms across his chest. "What does the color have to do with anything? It's not like being pink makes it any lighter!" They were still bickering as they left the room.

Emmy picked up the letter and read it again. It was such a weird thing to have. If only she knew why she had it. And if *he* was the one who had sent it.

The weather over the next few days was warmer than usual, which made the long walk to Latin Society a lot more cheerful. The wind died down enough to hear birds chirping, and Emmy even saw a few squirrels scampering between the trees. When she opened the cottage's secret door, Emmy saw fewer people than normal. A lot of people must be skipping society to take advantage of the weather. Brynn was there, and Emmy had already gotten her books out of her bag when she realized he wasn't alone. Jack's brother was with him, but it wasn't Malcolm…it was Vincent.

Emmy frowned. Why would Vincent be at Wellsworth? He had already graduated. He and Brynn had their heads close together, like they were talking about something they didn't want anyone else to hear, but that didn't make much sense. If they wanted to have a private conversation, a school society wasn't the best place to have it. Brynn looked up and saw Emmy watching them. He scowled, nodded his head at Vincent, and the two of them moved to the opposite side of the room. No one was sitting over there.

When she got back to the common room later that afternoon, Emmy sat next to Jack. "Hey, did you know Vincent's here?"

"Huh?"

"I saw him in Latin Society. He was talking with Brynn, and they definitely didn't want to be overheard."

Jack rubbed his forehead. "That can't be good."

"Yeah."

Jack leaned forward and started to whisper, "Vincent was Brynn's mentor in the Order. Maybe he still is, even though he's left school."

"Maybe," Emmy whispered. "In that case he might just be catching up with Brynn. That doesn't mean they're up to something."

Jack shrugged. He looked pretty skeptical. Before he could say anything else, Lola came into the common room and threw her bag down so hard it burst open and spilled her books all over the floor. She swore and started stuffing things back in the bag.

"What's up with you?" Emmy asked.

Natalie stomped into the room behind Lola and threw herself down in a chair. "Melina Bakas went hiking over the holidays and—"

"—and broke her bloody ankle," Lola interrupted.

"Ouch," Jack said.

"That's all you have to say!?" Lola exploded. "Our star striker is injured three weeks before the start of tournaments, and all you can say is 'ouch'?"

Emmy winced. It had been months since she'd played soccer, but she still felt a pang of longing whenever anyone talked about the game. "What are you going to do?" Jack asked.

Natalie sighed. "Dillon and Manuela are both good forwards—one of them will move to striker, I guess. One of our bench players will move up to regular, and we'll have to find someone else to take their place on the bench. We need fifteen players, so we'll have a tryout for the open spot."

Something fluttered in Emmy's chest. *An open spot.* And just for a benchwarmer. This team was a lot better than her team back home, but she might be good enough to sit on the bench.

But what about her mom? Emmy tapped her knuckles on the table. *No soccer.* Her mom had forbidden it.

But she's not here.

"When are tryouts?" she asked as casually as she could.

"Saturday."

It was ten o'clock on Saturday morning, and Emmy was shivering on the sidelines of the football pitch. She hadn't even been near a soccer ball in months. What if she wasn't good enough? What if she made a complete moron out of herself in front of the whole school? And what if… What if her mother found out somehow?

Lola ran over to her with a funny look on her face. "You're trying out?"

Emmy nodded.

"Have you… I mean…you *have* played football before, right?"

"Of course, I have!" Emmy said a little louder than she meant to.

"Okay, okay," Lola said, "just be prepared."

"For what?"

Lola bit her lip. "It'll be a tough trial."

Emmy's shoulders slumped. "You don't think I should do it." It wasn't a question. It was a statement of fact.

"I didn't say that." Lola put her arm around Emmy's

shoulder. "Close your eyes. Now think of the absolute worst thing that could happen to you today. Tripping over your cleats. Scoring on the wrong net. Trying to do a header and bashing the ball off your nose instead. Just picture all that blood dripping down your face."

"How is that supposed to help?"

Lola grinned. "Because when you prepare for the absolute worst, nothing can be as bad as what you've imagined." The whistle blew, and Lola took her spot on the pitch.

"Don't bet on it," Emmy grumbled.

Each girl had five minutes of playing time to show what they could do. Many of them were good, although not as good as Emmy had expected. Some looked like they had potential, but they weren't doing enough to showcase their skills. They weren't being aggressive, and that was the only way to stand out from the crowd.

"Hey, Emmeline!" called a voice from the stands. Emmy looked back and scowled. It was Victoria. "Remember, you're trying to get the ball *in* the net, not over top!"

A few people snickered, and Emmy felt her body stiffen.

"Did you bring your cheerleader pom-poms with you?" Victoria asked. "Give me an L! Give me an O! Give me an L-O-S-E-R!"

Emmy kept staring at the pitch. She would *not* let Victoria get to her. Not today.

There was no way she was leaving this pitch with people thinking she didn't know how to play soccer. The whistle blew, and the coach turned toward the sidelines.

"Willick!" she called. "You're up!"

Emmy ran to her position. She could hear Victoria teasing her, but she didn't care. Victoria didn't matter anymore. The only thing that mattered was getting the ball in the net.

The whistle blew again, and Emmy took off. A girl was moving the ball up the pitch, but she wasn't paying enough attention to where Emmy was. Emmy slid her foot in front of the girl's and pulled the ball backward. It was hers. She spun around and flew in the opposite direction. Lola was gunning straight for her, and Emmy slowed down to watch her footwork. Then she slid the ball between Lola's legs and met it on the other side. She dodged the next midfielder and picked up her speed. This was where she belonged. Her heart was meant to pound with the rhythm of fast feet. Her lungs were meant to feel like they might burst open with the very next step. No matter where she was in the world, the smell of freshly cut grass meant she was home.

Natalie was waiting in the defensive zone, but after months

of watching her play, Emmy knew how to attack. She faked left to force Natalie to her weak side, then circled around on her right. She reached her foot back and kicked the ball as hard as she could. The keeper dove, but it was way too late; the ball was in the back of the net.

Emmy turned around and stopped dead. Every person in the stadium was staring at her. It was quiet enough to hear a pin drop. All of Lola's worst-case scenarios raced through Emmy's head. She must have gone for the wrong net or broken some English soccer rules. She should have checked to make sure all the rules were the same.

"Red side, one–nil!" the coach called, and Emmy breathed out. At least she'd hit the right net.

The next few minutes of play were a lot tougher, but Emmy held her own. She had never played with a team this skilled; it was amazing. By the time the coach blew the whistle, Emmy didn't want to stop.

"Thanks very much, girls," the coach said. "The team and I will discuss things, and the captain will let you know when a decision has been made."

Emmy was halfway to the changing room when Lola caught up with her.

"Hey," Lola said. She had a weird expression on her face,

like she was trying to stop from busting at the seams. "What was that?"

Emmy groaned. She knew it. She *had* done something stupid. "What? What did I do?"

Lola exploded. "What did you do? You got past three of our best players and faked out our keeper, that's what! Where did you learn to play football like that?"

Emmy's face felt suddenly hot. She shrugged. Lola's face looked like it would burst with anger and joy all at the same time.

"Aren't you supposed to be meeting with the rest of the team?" Emmy asked.

Lola smirked. "It was a short meeting; the captain's right behind me."

A tall sixth year named Manuela was walking toward them with a grin plastered on her face.

"It's Willick, right?" she asked.

Emmy nodded.

"Good. Hope you like playing striker, 'cause you're starting our next match."

Emmy's mouth fell open. "I thought...I thought you were just looking for a benchwarmer."

"Something tells me you don't spend a lot of time on the bench," Manuela said with a wry smile.

"But—"

"We'll have practices every day this week to break you in," Manuela went on. "See you on the pitch tomorrow, right?"

"Uh, right."

Manuela grinned and walked away. Emmy's stomach jumped in a hundred directions. Being chosen was a huge honor, but it also scared her half to death. She'd have to face some really tough teams, and playing striker automatically made you a leader—and a target.

Lola put her arm round Emmy and dragged her away from the pitch. "Come on, let's go celebrate."

Emmy felt light-headed. *Striker?* "I didn't think I'd be starting," she said.

"Would you rather sit on the bench and watch?"

"No!"

"Then what's the problem?"

"Uh…" What could she say? *Well my mom forbade me from playing, but I tried out anyway. Sorry I totally screwed up your whole team.*

Emmy could see the look on her mother's face if she ever found out. She'd be furious…livid…*hurt*. She'd be crushed if she knew Emmy was lying to her. But not playing soccer…that hurt, too. And if her mother didn't care what Emmy wanted, why should she care what her mom wanted?

"No," Emmy said, "there's no problem." What her mother didn't know wouldn't hurt her.

CHAPTER 11

The Field Trip

The day after soccer tryouts, Emmy saw her mom's number appear on her phone. She winced and pressed the green button with a shaking finger. "Hi, Mom."

"Hi, darling. How are you?"

Emmy swallowed. She didn't want her voice to crack. "I'm good."

"How were your first few days of new classes?"

"Good. I still have humanities from last semester, that one runs all year, and I moved into second-year Latin."

"I'm so proud of you, honey. It seems like you're doing so well at school!"

"Thanks, Mom."

"It's a good thing you haven't had any distractions at Wellsworth. I think that's made a really big difference."

Emmy's cheeks felt hot. *Please don't ask about after-school stuff, please don't ask about after-school stuff!*

"Are you still going to that Latin club?"

"Uh, yep." She shuffled her feet. They were getting dangerously close to talking about soccer. "So, Mom, how's the TV show going?"

Her mom sighed. "Oh, well, it's fine, I guess. Lots of long days. I think they picked the most difficult people because they'd be the most entertaining." Her mom laughed, but it seemed to get caught in her throat. "Anyway, I have to run. I just wanted to check in and see how you're doing."

"Thanks." She paused. "I mean it, Mom. Thanks for calling."

"I love you, Em."

"I love you, too."

The next day, Emmy found a crowd of people standing outside her humanities class. Lola tried the door; it was locked.

"Maybe Barlowe is sick," Jack said.

"Let's hope so," Victoria said, and Arabella squealed with laughter.

"No such luck, Miss Stuart-Bevington."

Arabella smothered her mouth and Emmy grinned. Master Barlowe had arrived.

"Time for a field trip!" he announced.

A few people groaned.

"Don't worry, we're not going far," Barlowe said. "There's something on the other side of the grounds we need to see."

Victoria raised her hand. "Sir, I didn't wear walking shoes today, so I don't think I can—"

"Any shoes that conform to our school's uniform code should provide ample support for a walk of this nature," Barlowe said brightly.

Emmy smirked. Victoria's flimsy little slippers were definitely not uniform code.

Barlowe led them through the winding humanities hallways and out a little door Emmy had never seen before. They trudged along an overgrown path, past the old chapter house, past the headmaster's home, and past the teachers' housing. The path rose steadily, and Victoria moaned the whole way.

"Bet you wish you had my football cleats now," Emmy whispered.

Victoria glared at her. Emmy's soccer skills had been a blow to Victoria, and Emmy tried not to rub it in...too much.

"Master Barlowe," said Jaya, "where exactly are we going?"

"The Parish Church of Saint Felix," he said. "Otherwise known as our round-tower church."

"What's that?" Emmy asked.

"Round-tower churches were mostly built by the Normans and Anglo-Saxons," Barlowe explained. "This one is Anglo-Saxon, which makes it extremely old. They used the only stone they could find: flint. Flint isn't strong enough to build square corners, so the Saxons and Normans built round bell towers rather than having expensive stone blocks shipped in. You can still find round-tower churches all over Norfolk."

"Are we still in Norfolk, then?" Victoria muttered as she teetered behind the group. "I thought we must be halfway to Newcastle by now."

The path was getting steeper and sandier. The closer she got to the top of the hill, the more the wind whipped at Emmy's face.

Barlowe was the first to get to the top. "There." He pointed to something in the distance, and Emmy scrabbled up behind him. The church looked too narrow to stand up. Bits of stone lay here and there, like it had been flaking off for a long, lonely time. Its roof was made of some kind of black straw and was so steep it looked like it should slide right off the nearby cliffs that tumbled into the North Sea. Looming above it was a skinny round tower, its bell tinkling faintly in the breeze.

"Is it safe to go inside?" Emmy asked.

"Oh yes," Barlowe said, "it's perfectly safe. It might not be much to look at, but it is meticulously maintained."

"Are you sure?" Victoria asked. She was still huffing and puffing her way up the hill.

Barlowe smiled. "Positive."

Crumbling tombstones leaned into the path. They were overgrown with snaking yellow grass that licked at Emmy's ankles and made her shiver. This place was eerie.

Barlowe stopped in the arched entryway and waited for everyone to catch up. "Before we go in, let me remind you that this building and all its contents are irreplaceable. It has stood for over a thousand years, withstanding gales, plagues, and wars. I don't want to tell the headmaster that a third-year humanities class was able to bring it down. It is a sacred place. You *will* respect that.

"You may spend the rest of this class looking around and

asking me whatever questions you like. I expect a full report on my desk by Thursday afternoon."

The inside wasn't at all what Emmy had imagined. Instead of dark, crumbling stone, the walls were covered in bright white plaster that reflected light and shadows from long arched windows. She crouched next to a wide stone bowl. "What's this?"

"It's called a font," Barlowe said. "It's used for baptisms."

Emmy ran her hands along the sides. There were figures carved into the stone, but their faces were missing, like someone had taken a hammer to them. "What happened to the faces?"

"That font was built by medieval Catholics," Barlowe said. "The figures were destroyed by people trying to wipe Catholicism out of existence. People were using religion to gain power—it was an ugly time in our history."

"I'm glad that's over with," Emmy muttered.

Barlowe looked at Emmy with a rueful smile. "There will always be people who crave power, Miss Willick. And people who will go to any lengths to hold on to it." He motioned to the far side of the church. "There are a few relics and artifacts in a glass case on the north side of the church—and don't forget to look around the belfry. There are stairs on the inside that go all the way to the top, but they're closed off, so your best view will be from outside."

Emmy wandered up the aisle and ran her hand along the old wooden benches. A thousand years old. How many people had been to services here? How many weddings had been performed? How many funerals?

"A bit creepy in here, don't you think?" Lola whispered.

Emmy nodded. "But it's kind of peaceful, too."

Jack was standing at a glass display case, staring at all the artifacts. Emmy peered inside. Some of the objects were so old she didn't even know what they were. She was about to walk away when she saw an old letter at the very end of the case. She looked closely at the smudged writing. Maybe it was sent by a king or some other powerful figure.

Then she saw the signature. An icy chill inched down her spine, freezing her to the stone floor.

"What are you looking at?" Lola asked.

Emmy didn't say anything. She *couldn't* say anything.

"Hey, what's up with you?" Lola said.

"Master Barlowe," Emmy finally said, "why is this letter here?" Her voice sounded strange to her, like someone was grasping at her throat.

"It was found during an early twentieth-century restoration," Barlowe explained. "It's dated 1808, so the school wanted to preserve it."

"And the signature," she said, "does anyone know who that is?"

Barlowe looked at it and waved his hand dismissively. "Just a random student or teacher, I'm sure. Now, have a look at this copper shard." He steered everyone to the other side of the display case. "It's from an Anglo-Saxon shield…"

Emmy stopped listening. There was nothing random about this signature. She'd seen it before.

"Why do you keep staring at that old letter?" Lola hissed.

"Look at the signature," Emmy whispered.

Lola and Jack leaned in closer. Stamped under the signature was a skull with a cross on the right and a dagger on the left.

"Must have belonged to someone in the Order," Jack whispered.

"Okay, fine," Lola said, "who cares—"

"Not the symbol. The name."

At the bottom, just above the skull, the letter was signed, "Your Brother Loyola."

CHAPTER 12

Brother Loyola

Miss Willick?"

Emmy jumped.

"Miss Willick, are you all right?" Master Barlowe was staring at her like she was about to be sick. She *was* about to be sick. The room was spinning, and her stomach lurched like she had run too many wind sprints. Barlowe looked at the signature and something in his expression changed. As if he knew—really knew—what she was looking at. He glanced back at Emmy and the strange expression was gone. Maybe she'd just imagined it.

"Perhaps you should go to the medical center."

"No," Emmy said, "I think I just need to lie down."

"Very well, but take Ms. Boyd and Mr. Galt with you in case you need some assistance."

Emmy stumbled to the door and took a deep breath of salty air. *Just get back to Audrey House. One foot in front of the other*.

The common room was empty when they got there; most classes were still in session. Emmy sat on the edge of the nearest chair and rubbed her face.

"Do you want some water or something?" Jack asked.

Emmy shook her head. She just needed to think. Two letters. Both written in different centuries. "How can those two letters have the same signature?"

"Maybe that letter in the church was written by a relative," Lola suggested. "Maybe the name runs in your family."

"Maybe," Emmy said.

"You really don't know anything about your dad's family?"

"Nothing," Emmy said. "I'd never even seen anything that belonged to him until I found this box in the attic."

"What kind of box?" Jack asked.

Emmy bit her lip. She hadn't shown anyone the box. That

first letter she'd gotten had said to keep it safe. But Jack and Lola had accepted her in a way no one else ever had. If it wasn't safe with them, it wasn't safe with anyone.

"Come on."

They followed her up the stairs. Even Jack didn't hesitate to go into her room this time. He must have known how important this was to Emmy. She reached past the dust bunnies and old socks under her bed, pulled out the box, and put it on the table. She opened the lid and started arranging the medallions.

Lola whistled. "When you said you found a box in your attic, this wasn't exactly what I'd pictured."

"Do you know what those things are for?" Jack asked.

Emmy shook her head and started moving the medallions around. "I thought they might be some kind of puzzle, but I can't figure out how they fit together."

Lola leaned over the table and scrunched up her forehead. She moved a few pieces around and finally put two together. "These ones have matching lines. You see that?" She pointed to a place where the lines seemed to meet. "Almost like the hilt of a knife."

Emmy looked closer. She'd seen a hilt like that before.

"This might be the blade of the knife." Jack added another piece on top.

Emmy's stomach dropped. It wasn't just a knife. It was a dagger. She started pushing more pieces together, shuffling and reshuffling until an image started to form. She put the last two pieces in and fit them together like a cross. Instead of random medallions, they now made up a skull with a cross on the right and a dagger on the left.

The symbol for the Order of Black Hollow Lane.

"These were your dad's?" Jack finally asked. He sounded like someone was pinching his windpipe.

Emmy nodded.

"Then he must have been a student here," Jack said. "And he must have been a member of the Order."

Emmy sat down on the edge of the bed. Her dad was part of the Order of Black Hollow Lane…just like Jack's dad. "Hey, do you think your dad knew my dad? If they were both part of the Order, maybe—"

"I don't think it's a good idea to let anyone know your dad was part of the Order. You're not even supposed to know it exists. Besides, my dad wouldn't talk about it anyway. Membership is a supposed to be a secret, and he'd flip if I started asking questions."

"Do you know who Brother Loyola is?" Emmy asked.

"Not a clue." Jack picked up one of the medallions. "So, I

guess if your dad went to Wellsworth, that explains why your mom sent you here."

"I guess so. I wish I could ask her more about it, but she freaks out any time I bring up my dad. It's like she doesn't even want to remember him." She sighed. "I wouldn't have even found this box if someone hadn't sent me a letter telling me about it. I just wish I knew why."

Lola flung herself back onto Victoria's bed. "This guy's starting to tick me off. Why all the secrets? Why not send these letters with a return address? Better yet, why doesn't this mystery person just come right out and tell you stuff instead of just hinting at it all?"

"Maybe it's some kind of game," Jack said.

Emmy's jaw went tight. "Yeah, well, if it's a game, it's not much fun."

Jack and Lola looked at her.

"I'm tired of playing guessing games about my dad. I want to know something real about him, and I want to know if he's still…" Her voice cracked.

"…if he's still alive?" Jack finished. Emmy nodded. The bell rang out across the school grounds.

"We'd better get to football practice," Lola said. "Coach'll kill us if we're late."

Emmy couldn't focus at football practice, and she barely ate any supper. She couldn't think about anything but her father, the box, and its connection to her school. *His* school.

Study session seemed to take forever that night. She read the same sentence over and over. "This is pointless," she whispered to Jack and Lola. "I could be doing something useful right now." She glanced at Madam Boyd, who was busy with another student, then quietly got out her laptop.

"What are you doing?" Jack whispered.

"I'm going to see if there are any lists of school alumni online."

Jack shifted in his chair. "Uh, I don't think that's what Madam Boyd wants us to be working on right now."

"If she asks, I'll just say it's for an assignment."

Jack raised his eyebrows and Lola gave him a wry smile. "I think you've been a bad influence on her, Jack."

"ME!?" Jack hissed. "You're the one—"

"Oh, relax," Lola said. "It's no big deal if she misses one night of studying."

But it wasn't just one night. The next day Emmy skipped Latin Society so she could research online again. Soon she started wandering the school at random, missing tutorials and skipping society meetings. She lay awake at night, imagining her dad attending classes in the humanities wing or studying in the library. If she could just find *something* that connected him to Wellsworth, then she could focus on her schoolwork again.

Over the next week, Emmy searched every building she could get access to. She looked at every trophy, every plaque, and every picture on every wall. But there was no evidence of Thomas Allyn anywhere.

Emmy's next football practice didn't go very well. Lola seemed to be torn between empathy and irritation, and Emmy knew which emotion would win out in the end.

"I know this stuff with your dad is rattling you, but you've got to keep your head in the game." Lola banged the locker room door open. "Our first tournament is only a week away."

"I know." Emmy started unlacing her cleats.

"You're still getting used to our style of play. We have to gel together, otherwise—"

"I said, I know!" Emmy snapped.

Lola tossed her cleats into her bag and muttered something under her breath.

Emmy rubbed her eyebrows. "Look, I'll be better next time. I'm just distracted."

Lola snorted. "No kidding. Look, what do you think all this research you're doing is going to prove?"

"I don't know." Emmy slowly unzipped her gym bag. "I just want to know something about my dad."

"But..." Lola looked warily at Emmy. "But let's say you do find out more about him—then what? Just knowing won't bring him back."

Emmy ripped her socks off and stuffed them into her bag. Of course she knew her dad wasn't coming back. "Lola, I'm not stupid."

"I didn't say you were stupid, I just—"

"And you can stop trying to talk me out of finding him, because I'm not going to stop until I do!" Emmy grabbed her towel and marched toward the showers.

"You mean find out *about* him, right?" Lola said softly.

Emmy spun around. "What?"

"You said you won't stop until you find *him*."

Emmy stared back at her. "I know he's not coming back."

Lola picked up her bag and threw it over her shoulder. "Sometimes I'm not sure if you do."

Tears started prickling at the corners of her eyes, and Emmy blinked them furiously away. "I just want to know something about him, Lola. I don't even know what color his hair was."

"I know, but—"

"No, you don't know!" Other players were staring at them now, but Emmy didn't care. "You still have a dad, so you don't know anything about it!"

Lola threw her bag back down on the bench. "Hey, it's no picnic having my dad three hundred miles away!"

"I wouldn't care if my dad was three thousand miles away if I could still talk to him! If you want to know something about your dad all you have to do is pick up the phone! I can't even ask my mom because she's hidden everything about him my entire life!"

"So, what are you yelling at me for when they're the ones you're mad at?"

Lola picked up her bag and stormed out of the changing room. Emmy sat on the bench for a long time. Then she put her towel in her bag and walked back to Audrey House alone.

CHAPTER 13

Thomas Allyn

On Friday night, Emmy saw Jack and Lola sitting together in the common room. She hesitated, then went upstairs. She knew she should apologize to Lola. She also knew she wasn't ready to do it. She pulled out her phone and dialed her mom's number.

"What a lovely surprise!" her mom said. "But I can't talk long, I'm on my way to the airport."

"Okay, I just had a question. Why did you send me to Wellsworth?"

"Honey, we've been through this. I couldn't leave you alone while I was filming, and—"

"No, I mean, why did you choose Wellsworth? Why not some other school in England or a boarding school in the States?"

"Oh." The phone was silent. "I used to know someone who went there, and they really loved it."

Emmy's heart started beating a little faster. "Who was it?"

"Just someone I met when I lived in England—a friend."

"How did you meet this person?"

Her mom took a long time to answer. "In the university library. He was always there really late at night...like I was. I had to work during the day to cover my tuition costs, so I always did schoolwork at night."

Emmy swallowed hard. She'd never heard that story before. "Did you know right away that you would be...friends?"

"Not right away. Sometimes it takes a while for a friend-ship to develop."

"Do you ever miss that friend?"

"I..." Something crinkled on the end of the line. "I'm sorry, Em. I have to go."

"Wait, Mom, I—"

"No, I can't talk, I have a… I mean, we're almost at the airport. I'll talk to you later."

Emmy heard a beep and the phone went dead. She rubbed away a tear that was dribbling down her chin. She'd never heard her mom talk that way about her dad. Like a real person and not just an old relic to be forgotten.

She took out her dad's box and stared at the medallions. Maybe there was some clue here she was missing, something that would lead her to her dad. But the more she stared, the more lonely she felt. She had no idea what to do next.

She walked back downstairs to the common room and saw Natalie and Jaya walking out the door.

"Hey," Emmy called, "wait up!"

Natalie and Jaya turned around.

"Where are you guys going?" Emmy asked.

"We're meeting our lab partners to finish a chemistry report," Jaya said. "Maybe we can meet up later?"

"Sure." Emmy turned around and sighed. There weren't a lot of people in the common room that she knew that well… other than Jack and Lola. Finally, she walked over to their table. She was still annoyed at Lola, but sitting with her and Jack was better than being alone in her room. She sat down and glanced at Lola, then quickly looked away.

Jack sat in between them, drawing. Every once in a while, he would look at one of them, sigh loudly, and shake his head.

Emmy pursed her lips. Maybe if she could get him talking he would stop giving them irritating hints. She pointed at his drawing. "What's that?"

"Cadel's band is having a concert in a few weeks, and they asked me to do a poster."

Emmy peered closer; the poster was pretty incredible. Each band member was represented by a stylized silhouette that seemed to be dancing across the page. "How did you come up with that?"

Jack shrugged. "I don't know. I've always liked doing stuff like this."

"That's really cool. Doesn't your dad do something with art, too?"

Jack didn't look up, but his pencil slowed and his back got stiff. "He's an art and antiquities dealer. Music posters definitely aren't his thing."

"But isn't he proud that his son is an artist?"

Jack laughed. "Proud? More like humiliated. Artists don't make money, art *dealers* do. They make money by ripping artists off. So, he's pretty much mortified that his son might be an artist."

Emmy winced. She glanced across the room, where

Malcolm was sitting with a bunch of his friends. He and Jack were both part of Edmund House, and they barely even spoke. "Guess I'm not the only one with a messed-up family."

Lola glanced at her.

"I guess sometimes it just doesn't feel like I have a family at all," Emmy said.

Jack stopped drawing and looked at Emmy. "Of course, you have a family!"

Emmy cocked her head. "I do?"

Lola laughed and pointed at Jack, then at herself. "Duh, it's us!"

Emmy giggled, then she felt something catch in her throat. It was true. They really had become like her family. She swallowed hard and smiled again.

"Look," Lola said, "I know you're still mad about what I said, but—"

"No, you were right. I know I must seem crazy."

"Not crazy," Lola said. "Just mildly obsessed."

Emmy laughed. "Yeah, maybe. I just wish I could find out something about him."

Jack bit his lip. "Look, I know all of this is really important, but I saw the mark you got on that humanities quiz Barlowe gave back today."

Emmy felt her face get hot. She'd never gotten a grade that low before. "It was just a quiz."

"I know," Jack said, "but if you don't start getting your schoolwork done, you might get kicked out."

Emmy hunched back in her chair. It wasn't just humanities. Her grades had been slumping in all her classes. "I just can't seem to concentrate with this hanging over my head."

Nobody said anything. What was there to say? Emmy was *stuck*. Maybe she would have to give up on finding out anything about her dad.

Lola banged her hand on the table. "Right, that's it, then."

"Huh?" Emmy said.

"If you can't focus until you learn more about your dad, we're just going to have to get the information you need."

Emmy laughed. "And how exactly are we going to do that?"

"By breaking into the records in the school office."

Jack whipped around so fast his papers flew off the table. "Are you out of your mind? We can't break into the office!"

"Of course, we can," Lola said. "They keep records about students' families, their transcripts, all that stuff."

"Do you have any idea how many detentions we'd get for that?" Jack whispered. "We'd never see the light of day!"

Lola rolled her eyes. "Only if we get caught! And I have no intention of getting caught."

"No one ever intends to get caught!" Jack said. "Do you think every bank robber who ends up in jail started their days by saying, 'Gee, I think I'm going to get caught today'?"

"Well, if they're stupid enough to rob banks, they may as well have been trying to get caught!"

Jack looked at Emmy. "Would you please tell her that this idea is completely insane?"

Emmy didn't say anything, and Jack's eyes went wide. "You can't actually be considering this!"

Emmy tapped her foot against the table. It *was* insane. They could be expelled. Hadn't she just called them her family? And now she was thinking about doing something that could get them all separated forever.

But she was already separated from her dad. As separate as two people could be. If there was information about him in the school office, it could be the bridge she'd always wanted. *Needed*.

"Let's do it."

"This is completely mental," Jack said.

"Shh!" Lola whispered. "Are you trying to get us caught? Just shut it, already!"

Emmy looked over her shoulder. No one seemed to have noticed them leaving Audrey House after curfew, but she didn't want to take any chances.

"Can we go a little faster, please?" Jack whispered. "I'm going to freeze out here!"

"Stop being such a baby!" Lola hissed.

Emmy pulled the collar of her coat up around her chin and walked a little faster. The outside lights were way too bright for a stealth mission. It'd be a miracle if they didn't get caught. Her teeth were chattering so loudly the headmaster could probably hear them from inside his house.

They finally reached the main building, and Lola eased open a door. Floodlights hissed and sputtered, filling the hallways with a hazy green light. Slowly, carefully, they crept through the corridors until they reached the office.

Lola stuck a couple of hairpins inside the keyhole. A minute went by. Then two. The door was still locked.

"Can't you go any faster?" Jack whispered.

"Not if you keep bothering me," Lola muttered. "I've only done this a few times."

"Oh, move over." Jack grabbed the pins out of Lola's hand.

Lola rolled her eyes. "Yeah, right, like you're going to be able to—"

Click. The door swung open.

Jack looked up and flashed them a grin in the misty green light.

"How did you do that?" Lola asked.

"Having shady older brothers isn't always a bad thing," he said. "Malcolm and Vincent could break into the National Gallery if they ever got the idea in their heads."

The office was deserted. Emmy reached for the computer at the main desk, but Lola pulled her back. "Somebody might see us there. Let's go to Mrs. Hughes's desk, it's around the corner."

They crept to the very last desk and Jack flicked on the computer.

"You know, I could have gotten the lock myself," Lola muttered. "I almost had it."

"You had those pins jammed in so far I thought they might never come out."

The sound of the computer whirring to life drowned out Lola's suggestion of where Jack could put those pins.

Emmy sat down and tapped her fingers on the desk. "You're sure your mom's password will work on this computer?"

"I've seen her use it on office computers before," Lola said. "It'll work."

Emmy typed it in and pressed her lips together. Icons popped onto the screen. Her heart started beating a little faster. Internet browser…newsletters…inbox…

"There!" Jack pointed to a corner of the screen. "Student Records."

Emmy opened it. There were hundreds of files inside, all labeled by year. "I don't know how old he is, but apparently he and my mom were in college at the same time, which means he must have been here about twenty years ago."

She clicked on the file and found hundreds of new ones. These ones were all labeled by name. Genevieve Abrams, Rhys Algernon, Vivian Beaufort. No Thomas Allyn.

She checked the next year, then the next, and then another. No Thomas Allyn. Her shoulders slumped. "He's not here."

"Try working backward," Lola suggested. "Maybe nineteen years ago."

Emmy tried nineteen, then eighteen. Marilyn Acles. John Addington. Thomas Allyn. Her heart stopped. "That's him." She steadied her hand and clicked on the file. "Thomas Edward Allyn. Born in King's Lynn. Parents' Names: Edward and Emmeline Allyn. Died in… Wait, that can't be right."

"What can't be?" Jack asked.

"It says he died in—"

Lola held up her hand, her eyes were as wide as saucers. "Someone's coming!"

She pushed the power button on the computer, and they all dove under the desk. A few seconds later the office door clicked open.

"Hello?" a deep voice called out. "Anyone there?"

Emmy held her breath. Thank goodness Lola suggested a computer at the back of the room.

"Must have been hearing things," the man muttered. The door banged shut and the man's footsteps died away.

Emmy looked at Lola. Was it safe to come out? "Let's get out of here," Lola whispered.

They tiptoed back into the hallway, and Jack locked the door behind them. The entrance hall was dark and silent; it looked like the coast was clear.

"That was way too close," Emmy whispered.

"It would have been fine if you two had kept your voices down," Jack hissed.

"Actually, I saw you on the security camera," said a deep voice from the end of the hall.

It was Jonas. "I think it's time we have a little chat."

CHAPTER 14

Trouble

Jonas led them down a long staircase. Emmy gripped the railing to stop her knees from giving out. What would their punishment be? Detention every Saturday until the end of term? A weeklong suspension? *Please, don't let us get expelled!*

Jonas unlocked a door and flicked on a lamp that left most of the room still dark. "So, who's going to tell me what that was all about?"

Emmy stared at her shoes. It was her fault they were here. Jack didn't even want to come. She couldn't let her friends go down with her. "You see, Sir, I—"

"It's my fault," Jack said.

Emmy gasped. What was Jack doing?

"It was my idea to break into the office," he continued. "I wanted to look something up on the computer."

Emmy looked at Lola, who was staring straight ahead, her expression completely blank.

"Jack, what are you—"

"Don't try and cover for me, Emmy," Jack interrupted. "I was the one who broke into the office. I'm sure the security cameras caught me picking the lock."

Jonas nodded, and Emmy stared at Jack. She couldn't let him do this. "No, I—"

"I was the one who actually broke in," Jack cut in, "so I'm the one who should get in trouble."

Jonas eyed Jack carefully. "I'm quite sure it was Miss Willick who was sitting at the computer."

"She was looking up something for me. She's much better with computers than I am, so I asked her to do it for me. She didn't want to, but I kinda made her."

Emmy opened her mouth, but Lola stepped on her toes.

"I see," Jonas said. "And what was it she was looking up for you?"

"The midterm report being sent to my parents," Jack said. He didn't blink, he didn't shuffle his feet, he just stared into Jonas's eyes and told a bald-faced lie. "I haven't been doing so well this term, and I was afraid my parents would find out. I wanted to know what the teachers were going to tell them."

"I see," Jonas said again.

Jack bowed his head. "I know it was wrong. I've just been having such a hard time this term. I promise I won't do anything like this again, and I promise I'll try harder in class. But please, sir, don't tell my parents. They're worried enough as it is."

He sniffled. Lola snorted, then coughed to try and cover it up. Jonas gave Jack a shrewd look, then stood up. "I'll speak to your head of house about getting you some extra study sessions. It's Larraby, right?"

Jack nodded and looked up. His face was filled with so much contrition, Emmy didn't know whether to laugh or try and stop him.

"But no more nighttime wandering, or I'll have no choice but to report you," Jonas said. He opened the door and they all nodded as they shuffled out as quickly as they could.

Nobody said anything until they were safely in the common room. Lola threw herself down in a chair and burst out laughing. "I cannot believe you did that."

"I can't believe he bought it," Jack said.

"You shouldn't have done that," Emmy said. "Now you'll be stuck doing extra study sessions all term."

"Better than us all being chucked out," he said.

"Well, thanks," Emmy mumbled. *She* should be the one doing extra study sessions. *She* should be the one who had saved all their skins. When was she going to stop being such a chicken?

"I just wish we'd had time to see more of that file," Lola said.

"Yeah, well, I'm fresh out of excuses, so we're not going back," Jack said.

"But at least we got a bit of info on your dad," Lola said, clapping Emmy on the shoulder. "You're named after your grandmother—did you know that?"

Emmy shook her head. "There was one weird thing, though. There was a date of death beside his name."

"A date of death?" Jack asked.

"Yeah. The file said he died two years before I was born. Obviously that can't be right."

Lola shrugged. "Somebody probably mixed him up with someone else and put it in his file by mistake."

"Maybe," Emmy said. "We still don't know anything about Brother Loyola or why somebody sent me the letters."

"It's funny that they sent you a letter that's so similar to that old letter in the round-tower church," Jack said. "Do you think this person knew you'd compare them?"

"I haven't really compared them, actually," Emmy said. "I was so shocked by the signature I didn't really get a good look at the letter."

"Tomorrow's Sunday," Lola said, "which means the church will be open. Why don't you take another look?"

Jack yawned. "Just promise me you'll go during the day. I'm not doing any more midnight treks."

Emmy walked through the church's grassy tombstones and clutched at her scarf. She was getting used to the constant winds that whipped off the North Sea and through the school's grounds. The smell of the ocean was a lot stronger out here than it was in the middle of campus. The cliffs were so close she could hear the waves beating against them. There was something about the water that was both comforting and exotic. It felt like home, but a home that was exciting and always surprising her.

Lola was having lunch with her mom, and Jack had to meet with Larraby to schedule all the study sessions he was going to be stuck doing. Emmy was on her own.

She pushed open the rounded door and stepped into the church. "Hello?"

Nobody answered. She walked to the back of the church and looked at the glass display cases. There was the letter, old and faded, but with a clear signature at the bottom. *Your Brother Loyola.*

She took off her gloves and pulled her father's letter out of her coat pocket. The signature was the same.

Emmy squinted at the letter in the case. No, it *wasn't* the same signature. The words were the same, but the writing was definitely different. The letter in the case was written in large, loopy scrawls, but in her father's, the writing was thin and tightly spaced. The signatures looked really different. How could there be more than one Brother Loyola?

Brother. Not "brother" but "Brother" with a capital "B."

"It's not a name," she said under her breath, "it's a title. The title of the person in charge of—"

"Well, well, well," said a voice behind her. "If it isn't the Yankee redhead."

Emmy whirled around. Jack's old roommate Brynn was leaning against the baptismal font, staring at her with cold, black eyes.

"What brings you out here?" he asked her.

"Nothing," she said quickly. "Why, what are you doing here?"

"Oh, nothing." He smiled. A shiver ran up Emmy's spine. Brynn's smile looked anything but friendly.

"You should be careful," he said. "This building isn't all that safe."

Emmy's fingers started to twitch.

"Thousand-year-old stone and all that," he said. "Who knows what kind of accident could happen? I know everyone at Latin Society would be devastated if anything happened to our favorite member." He started walking toward her. "Haven't you figured out that we'd rather not have girls hanging around our club? We don't take kindly to them sticking their noses into our business."

"I'm not afraid of you," Emmy lied. She tried to back away but walked straight into a stone wall.

Brynn chuckled. "I know you American girls are taught to be strong and brave." He was only a few feet away now. "But that's a quality that can get you into trouble over here." He reached out and ripped the letter from her hand. "What's this? A letter from your boy—"

His voice trailed off. He was staring at the letter, eyes glued to the page. "Where did you get this?"

Emmy's heart gave a little jump. He must recognize the signature. "What do you care? It's my letter, give it back."

He looked up at her. His gaze was fierce. "Don't play games with me! Tell me where you got this letter!"

Emmy swallowed hard. She had to get out of here, but she also wanted that letter back. "It's mine." She reached forward and tried to grab it, but he leapt back.

"There's no way it's your letter!" he growled. "Tell me where you got it and tell me what you know about Brother Loyola!" The words caught in his throat and the letter shook in his hand.

"I don't have to tell you anything," she said. "You can't tell me what to do, I'm not a member of your stupid Order of Black Hollow Lane."

He shoved her hard into the wall. Pain shot through her back as she crunched into the hard stone. She tried pushing back, but he had her pinned.

"No one outside the Order is allowed to say that name," he

snarled. "Not even a stupid, arrogant American girl. Now tell me what you know about the things in this letter."

"Let me go," she yelled, "or I'll scream bloody murder until someone shows up."

"No one would hear you way out here. Even the teachers' housing is too far away." She pushed again, but Brynn just laughed. "Should have done more push-ups at football practice."

Emmy felt a jolt in her chest. He was right. Her arms weren't her strong point. If she was going to get out of here, she needed to use her legs.

Slowly she stopped struggling. She looked down at her shoes and sniffled. "All right, I'll tell you everything." Her voice quavered, and Brynn relaxed his grip. Emmy sprang forward and kicked him in the shins as hard as she could. He grunted and limped back, and Emmy launched her whole body into his. He crashed into the display case, and Emmy ran past him. She didn't look back when she heard him scrabbling to his feet. Once she was out the door, she'd be able to outrun him.

She didn't stop running until she made it all the way back to Audrey House. The common room was filled with people, all oblivious to the girl who was shaking and breathing like she'd been running for her life. She ran up to her room and leaned her head against the door. It felt like she *had* been running for her life.

She took a few deep breaths and rubbed the back of her neck. At least she'd gotten out of there without anything more than a sore back. At least he hadn't gotten any information out of her. She gasped.

The letter. Brynn still had her father's letter.

Emmy stayed in her room all afternoon. Thank goodness Victoria had gone home for the weekend; she couldn't deal with her now. She lay on her bed, stretching her back and thinking. The more she thought, the angrier she felt. Brynn assumed she was just a scared little girl. Well, maybe she was scared. But that didn't mean he could get away with attacking her and stealing one of her most prized possessions.

She clutched her dad's box and closed her eyes, as if it were some kind of charm that would give her an extra dose of bravery. *I can do this. I can do this.*

She went downstairs and found Jack and Lola. "Get your coats, we're going for a walk." She waited for them outside. She didn't want to run into Brynn in the common room. Not yet.

"We'd better not be stealing anything this time," Jack said as he opened the door and shrugged on his coat.

"It's nothing like that," she said.

"Nothing like what?" Lola quickly followed behind Jack.

"Nothing like theft, breaking and entering, or hacking," Jack said. "Wait, there's no hacking, is there?"

Emmy shook her head.

"Well, that's disappointing," Lola said. "So, what's up?"

Emmy took them down the forest path and launched into her story. The more she told, the more serious their faces looked. By the end, Jack's fingers were twitching, and he was tugging at his ear. But Lola looked surprisingly calm.

"So, you're telling me Brynn attacked you," Lola said, "then he stole your dad's letter."

Emmy nodded.

"Right, then." Lola spun on her heel and started walking back toward Audrey House. "Time for another family chat."

"Wait!" Emmy grabbed Lola's shoulder. "You can't just punch him again, you'll get in trouble."

"Who cares? He can't get away with this!"

"I don't want him to get away with it, either," Emmy said, "that's why we have to talk to him and convince him to give me back the letter."

Lola whipped around. "*Talk* to him? Talk to that weaselly

little git? Jack tried talking to him in first year and all it got him was a night out in the cold and a broken ankle."

"That was an accident!" Jack said.

Lola swore. "It's no accident when somebody pretends a friend is hurt so you go rushing out to look for them, then takes away your flashlight so you get lost in the forest, stumble around until you break your ankle, and have to spend the night in the bloody wilderness."

Emmy looked at Jack. "Is that what Brynn did?"

"He… I mean, yeah. The ankle thing was an accident, though. It's not like he meant for it to happen."

Emmy's chest felt heavy and hot. Who did Brynn think he was? He couldn't just attack people or get them lost in the forest and think he could get away with it. She'd had enough of him. She pushed past Lola and marched up the path.

"Where are you going?" Jack asked.

"I'm going to get my letter back!"

She ran back to the house, flung the door open, and scanned the room. Brynn was sitting in an armchair and seemed to be having a serious conversation with Malcolm. She walked straight toward Brynn as if Malcolm wasn't even there. He wasn't the Order member she wanted to see. "We're going to talk outside. Now."

Brynn raised an eyebrow, then followed her out the door to where Jack and Lola were waiting. He eyed Lola and lifted his chin. "I see I have a welcoming committee."

"Never mind them," Emmy said. "Give me my letter."

Brynn smiled. "I don't think so."

"Give me my letter, or I'll tell Boyd what happened. And if you give it back, I might be able to stop Lola from beating you up again, but I can't make any promises."

"You can drop the tough girl act, I'm not giving you that letter."

Emmy shrugged. "Fine, then I'll go to Madam Boyd and—"

"No, I don't think you will."

"I'm not afraid of you, Brynn." That wasn't exactly true, but he didn't need to know that. "Don't bother trying to intimidate me, because it won't work."

"If you tell Boyd about the letter, or about our 'conversation' in the church, I'll tell her that you broke into the school office and stole confidential student information."

Emmy froze. How could he possibly know about that?

"How do you—"

"You and your little friends aren't that good at covering your tracks," he said. "That security guard might have let you off easy, but once I finish telling the tale, all three of you will be on your way out of here."

Emmy felt the color drain from her face. Was he bluffing? Or could he really get all of them expelled? She folded her arms across her chest like nothing he said was rattling her. "Go ahead and tell. You can't prove it."

Brynn shrugged. "And you can't prove I was anywhere near the round-tower church today, let alone anything that happened there. I've got powerful people on my side. They'll make sure I'm taken care of."

"What, you mean the stupid Order?" Lola spat.

Brynn's face went hard, and he looked Jack straight in the eye. "You told them? You told them about the Order?"

"He didn't have to tell us," Emmy said, "we found a bunch of information in an old book. A book he tried to keep us from reading. But I had to learn everything I could about the Order once I found out that—"

Jack grabbed her arm and shook his head. He'd already warned her not to tell anyone her dad had been part of the Order.

"…once I found out that they were a secret society," Emmy finished.

The door opened, and Malcolm came out. Usually he seemed so easygoing, but the look on his face was anything but relaxed. "You shouldn't be talking about this stuff here."

"This is a private conversation," Jack said.

"Not when you're talking about the Order where anyone could hear you," Malcolm whispered. "You were talking so loud I could hear you through the door."

"So, you know what Brynn did?" Jack said. "You know he attacked Emmy and that he's threatening to get us expelled, and you're not going to do anything about it?"

Malcolm's face twitched, and he shuffled his feet. "Look, I don't like it much, either, but she's meddling in stuff that could get her into trouble. She just needs to back off, and everything will be fine."

"It's not fine," Jack said. "None of the stuff you guys do is fine."

"How would you know?" Malcolm said. "You didn't even give it a chance."

"Of course, he didn't," Brynn said, "he's too much of a chicken to even try. Face it, Malcolm. Your brother's nothing but a coward."

Emmy waited for Malcolm to defend Jack, or to at least tell Brynn to back off. But Malcolm didn't say anything. He looked at Jack with sad eyes, then walked back inside.

"It wasn't supposed to be like this," Brynn said to Jack. "We were supposed to be in this together. No wonder your family thinks you're such a disappointment." He threw the door open and disappeared inside.

"You okay?" Jack asked Emmy.

She nodded. "How about you?"

He shrugged. "I'm used to it." The look on his face made Emmy think he'd never get used to it.

"Well, I guess that's that." Emmy leaned against the stone wall of the house. "I just wish I could get my letter back. It totally freaked Brynn out when he read it."

"I wonder why?" Jack asked. "I mean, people outside the Order aren't supposed to know about it, but I'm sure it slips out every once in a while. It doesn't seem to have hurt them yet."

"He kept asking me what I know about Brother Loyola. I think that must be the title for the leader of the Order. I bet that person is supposed to be a complete secret. I wonder who it is?"

"It's got to be Larraby, don't you think?" Lola said. "He runs the Latin Society, which is where they recruit a lot of people, right?" She looked at Jack, who nodded.

"And it's not like Larraby works that hard as a teacher," Emmy said. "He never does anything to help me learn Latin, even though he's supposed to."

"Don't take him too lightly," Jack warned. "If he is the head of the Order, he's no joke."

Emmy nodded and opened the door. They sat at a table in the corner for a while, but nobody said much. Finally, they all decided to go to bed.

Emmy lay awake a long time. Her back was still sore, and she couldn't get her mind to stop racing. Eventually she drifted off, lulled by the sound of the breeze rustling the trees.

CHAPTER 15

Eighteen Years Ago

Emmy had a lot to distract her from Brynn and the Order over the next few weeks. There were soccer tournaments every weekend now, and they were all leading up to the biggest one of the season: the East Anglian Football Championship. They'd be battling the best teams from three counties, and they were practicing every day. She was glad to have the distraction. She threw all her frustration onto the pitch, loving every minute she spent with the grass under her cleats. Nobody could get to her here, and she got to kick things for ninety minutes straight.

On the Monday before the championship, Lola shot out of humanities class the moment the bell rang. "Meet you on the pitch!"

Emmy shoved her books in her bag and was flinging it over her shoulder when Jonas walked in. "I think I found something of yours in the round-tower church, young miss."

Emmy's bag slipped off her shoulder. "You found my letter?"

"Letter? No, your gloves." Jonas pulled Emmy's gloves out of his pocket and handed them to her. "I found them on a pew and saw your name on the tag."

"Oh." Emmy's heart sank. She took the gloves out of his hand. "Thanks."

"Are you missing a letter, then?"

Emmy glanced behind her. Brynn was there, sitting a few rows back, going over something with Master Barlowe. "Yeah, I was in the church when...when I lost it."

"I wouldn't worry about it too much," Jonas said. "These things always turn up eventually." He gazed at Emmy, like he was trying to puzzle something out. "This letter...it must have been an important one?"

Emmy nodded, and Jonas scratched his chin. "I've learned a few things about finding missing items in eighteen years working at Wellsworth. Maybe I could help. I assume this letter was addressed to you?"

"Not exactly. It…" She broke off. Eighteen years. "Wait, you were a student before you started working here, right?"

"Sure," he said.

Emmy thought back to the first day they met, the day he told her she'd get over that overwhelming feeling. The feeling he still remembered even though he'd graduated almost twenty years ago. "You graduated eighteen years ago?"

"That's right."

Emmy's heart started pounding. "Then you must have known my dad!"

Jonas wrinkled his forehead. "Your father was at Wellsworth?"

"Yeah!" Jack had warned her not to say anything about her dad being part of the Order, but there was no harm in saying he went to Wellsworth. "He graduated eighteen years ago, too!"

"Excuse me, Emmy." Barlowe had appeared beside her. "Sorry to interrupt, but I need to go over something in the textbook with you."

"Sure, just a moment." She turned back to Jonas. "You must have known Thomas Allyn, right?"

The book slipped from Barlowe's hands and tumbled down a few steps. Jonas picked it up and handed it back to Barlowe, who looked strangely pale.

"You all right, mate?" Jonas asked.

Barlowe nodded. "Just clumsy."

Jonas put a hand on Barlowe's shoulder and turned back to Emmy. "So, Tom Allyn is your father, is he?"

"Yes! So, you knew him?" Emmy was shaking. How could she have forgotten that Jonas went to Wellsworth? She should have asked him weeks ago.

"A bit, yes," Jonas said. "I can't say we ever moved in the same circles, but I knew who he was. Bit of a troublemaker, I think. Good rugby player, though. That must be where you get your football feet."

A warm rush flooded Emmy's chest. *A rugby player*. "What else?"

Jonas shook his head. "Not much, I'm afraid. Like I said, I didn't really know him that well. So, what's he up to these days?"

Just like that, the warmth was gone. Emmy tucked her hair behind her ear and looked at her shoes. "Oh, he's...he's dead."

"I'm sorry to hear that," Jonas said gently.

"Yeah, well…" She scratched the back of her head. This was why she didn't tell people about her dad. Because every time she did, the conversation just seemed to fall off the edge of a cliff.

"Your last name isn't Allyn, though, is it?" Jonas asked.

Emmy shook her head. "I have my mom's last name." She looked down at her feet. She didn't really feel like explaining more.

"Well, thanks for bringing me my gloves, Jonas."

"No trouble." Jonas had a strange expression. Then he blinked and shook his head. "I'm sorry, young miss. I just… You just look a bit like him."

The warm tingle crept back into her chest. "Really?"

Jonas smiled, but he looked more sad than happy. "From what I can remember, which isn't much, I'm afraid. Anyway, I'd better get going."

He left, and Emmy looked at Barlowe, who still wasn't looking very well. "Was there something you wanted to speak to me about?"

"Oh, yes." Barlowe cleared his throat. "Actually, I think it can wait. You'd better get to football practice, or your coach will have my head for making you late."

Emmy didn't need to be told twice. Brynn glared at her as she ran past, but she didn't have time to worry about him now. She couldn't afford to be late; their coach was on the warpath these days. By the time practice ended, Emmy felt like she had run a marathon.

"If we keep this up we'll be too exhausted to get out of the first round," Lola said as they walked back to Audrey House after practice.

"I thought it was a great practice!" Emmy said, her feet bouncing along the path.

Lola snorted. "Who put the happy pills in your teacup?"

"Oh, no one," Emmy said, "I just found out that Jonas knew my dad, that's all."

Lola stopped walking and whipped Emmy around to look at her. "Huh?"

Emmy told Lola what happened. "He didn't remember much, but at least it was something. I can't believe I didn't think of asking him before."

Suddenly Lola slapped her forehead. "My mum!"

"What about her?"

"My mum was here right around then! Why didn't I think of asking her?"

"Wait, your mom was a student here?"

"Sure," Lola said, "loads of teachers were. They like hiring old students—keep it in the family and all that."

"Maybe there are more teachers who knew him!"

"Maybe," Lola said. "I'll ask my mum tonight."

Emmy looked at her watch and chewed on her thumbnail. Lola was having supper with her mom, and they should be back any minute. The common room door opened. Emmy jumped up, but she sat back down right away. It was just a couple of sixth-year girls.

Emmy sighed. She shouldn't get her hopes up. Lola's mom might not have even been at Wellsworth when her dad was here. Even if she had been, it was a big school, and their paths might never have crossed.

She looked at her watch again. She may as well get a start on her homework while she waited. She started rummaging in her bag when the door opened again. This time it was Madam Boyd. And she was walking straight toward Emmy.

"Miss Willick, I need to see you in my office immediately."

Emmy fumbled with the zipper of her bag and flung it over her shoulder. Madam Boyd was already walking through the door with Lola trailing behind. Emmy flashed Lola a grin, but Lola didn't smile back. In fact, she looked downright worried.

Butterflies started swirling in Emmy's stomach. What was going on? She hurried into the office and Lola closed the door behind them.

Madam Boyd leaned her cane against her desk and looked straight into Emmy's eyes. "Is Thomas Allyn your father?"

Emmy nodded.

Madam Boyd stared at her for a few seconds, then turned away and pressed a finger to her lips. "How is that possible?"

Emmy swallowed hard. "How is *what* possible?"

Madam Boyd looked back at Emmy. "The Thomas Allyn I knew died fifteen years ago. So how can he have a twelve-year-old daughter?"

"It was ten years ago. But I think there was a mistake with the records, because the computer—" Lola cleared her throat, and Emmy stopped talking. Mentioning that they had seen confidential school records was not a good idea. "—uh, I mean, there are other records that say he died fifteen years ago, but it was only ten."

Madam Boyd gave her a wry smile. "Then how could I have attended his funeral?"

Emmy shook her head. There couldn't have been a funeral for her dad fifteen years ago.

"It must be a different Thomas Allyn," Lola said. "It must not be the same person."

Emmy's heart deflated. Lola was right. It was the only explanation that made sense. But Madam Boyd was shaking her head. "Hazel eyes, freckles on the nose, bright-red hair... You look just like him."

Emmy sank into a nearby chair. "My dad had red hair?"

Madam Boyd limped a few steps and sat in the chair across from Emmy. "What do you know about your father?"

"Nothing."

"Nothing?" Madam Boyd repeated.

"Really, I don't know anything about him. He disappeared when I was three, and my mother won't talk about him. All I know for sure is his name."

Most people looked sad when Emmy said things like that. Most people looked sorry for her. But Madam Boyd didn't look sorry. She looked relieved. "Emmy, I need you to listen very carefully." She put her hand on the arm of Emmy's chair. "You cannot tell anyone who your father is."

Emmy twisted the bottom of her sweater. "Why not?"

"I know this is difficult for you, but I need you to promise."

"But—"

"Promise me you won't tell anyone."

"Can't you at least say why?" Lola asked, but Madam Boyd was already shaking her head.

"No, I can't. I can only imagine how frustrating this is. But I need you to trust me. No one can know that you are in any way connected to Thomas Allyn."

Emmy bit her lip. There hadn't been a lot of people in humanities class when she had asked Jonas about her dad. But Barlowe had been there, and Brynn had been only a few desks behind her. Maybe she should tell Madam Boyd. But if the thought of Emmy's dad made Madam Boyd this nervous, what would she do if she found out that people might already know?

"I need your word, Emmy," Madam Boyd said.

If Brynn had overheard her talking to Jonas, there was nothing she could do about it now. She slumped down in her chair and nodded. "Can't you tell me *something* about him? Anything?"

Madam Boyd pursed her lips, then silently shook her head.

Emmy got up and walked out the door. So much for getting answers.

Lola followed her up the stairs. "What was that all about?"

"I was hoping you could tell me. What did she say when you asked her about my dad?"

"The moment I said his name she spilled her coffee all over the table. I don't think I've ever seen her so freaked out."

They got to the third-floor landing, and Emmy leaned on one of the thick wooden windowsills. "Jonas said something about my dad causing trouble. I thought it must just be pranks or something like that, but maybe it was something else. Something more serious." A knot clenched in her stomach. She didn't really have any memories of her dad. Just a few vague images of someone who loved her. She'd always assumed he was a good person, but how could she really be sure?

CHAPTER 16

Confrontation

It was the morning of the East Anglian Football Championship, and Emmy's breakfast looked about as appetizing as canned cat food on toast.

"You've got to eat a proper meal," Lola said as she dumped more sausage on Emmy's plate.

Some kind of yellowish goo oozed out of one of the sausages. "How is this a proper breakfast?"

"Protein."

Emmy wrinkled her nose. "I think I'll stick with the eggs."

"And don't forget your carbs." Lola stuffed a bagel into Emmy's mouth. "Good for energy! You're going to need it if you're going to make it through all six matches today."

Emmy pulled the bagel out of her mouth as Natalie and Jaya joined them in the food line. Natalie was already wearing her soccer uniform.

"You nervous?" Jaya asked.

"Just a little," Emmy said. She'd never played six matches in one day. This was definitely the biggest tournament she'd ever been in.

"I would be, too," Jaya said. "That's why I never tried football."

Natalie snorted. "That and you wouldn't be caught dead in a smelly uniform."

Jaya made a face. "That, too."

"My tray's getting heavy, let's go sit down," Lola said to Emmy. "See you on the pitch, Nat."

Natalie and Jaya both smiled and kept piling food onto their plates.

"Hey, look who it is." Lola nodded her head toward a table. Jack's brother Vincent was sitting there, talking with some boys from Latin Society.

"What's he doing here again?"

Lola shrugged. "Maybe he really misses school."

"Enough to come up here on weekends? And I bet he had to miss work when I saw him at Latin Society. Nobody likes their old school that much."

They sat down at a table and Emmy ripped off a chunk of her bagel. There had to be some reason Vincent kept hanging around the school. But what?

Jack slid into a seat next to them. "Morning," he said glumly.

Emmy winced. Thanks to them breaking into the school office, Jack was being sent home for the weekend for extra study time.

"Did you see your brother's here?" Lola asked.

Jack nodded. "Yeah, I saw him talking to Malcolm yesterday. Hasn't bothered to say hi to me, though."

"Sorry," Emmy said.

Jack took a gulp of juice and rolled his eyes. "I'm used to it. Anyway, I was wondering," he leaned closer to Emmy, "that box of yours—could I get a closer look at it?"

"Sure. Victoria has some kind of club on Monday afternoons. You could come up to my room and—"

"Actually," he said sheepishly, "I was kind of hoping I might be able to take it home with me this weekend."

Emmy twisted her fingers together. Letting him look at it was one thing, but *giving* it to him to take home? She wasn't sure about that. "Um, what for?"

"My dad has loads of books about analyzing art and antiques," Jack said. "They talk about how to figure out what period an object is from, what its purpose was, and all that kind of stuff. I thought maybe if I took the box with me, I could find out more about it."

"I don't know if it's a good idea," Emmy said. "Your dad *belongs* to the Order."

"He's away on business right now," Jack said. "It's just my mom at home, and Malcolm's not coming along. Don't worry, it's totally safe."

"Well…" That *did* sound like a good idea. Emmy was definitely tempted. She hadn't found out anything new about her dad or the Order in weeks. But handing the box over to someone else wasn't something she was excited about, even if it was Jack.

"I understand if you don't want to," Jack said, but he did look a bit hurt.

"No, no, it's fine," Emmy said. She couldn't stand the idea of making his weekend even worse. At least this way he'd have something to do other than homework, and who knew? He might stumble across some useful information.

Jack grinned. "Great!"

Half an hour later, Emmy was in the common room, giving Jack a plain brown bag with the box inside. It felt like saying goodbye to a friend.

"I'll treat it like gold," Jack promised.

Something twanged in Emmy's chest, but she ignored it. It wasn't like she was handing over her firstborn child. It was just a box.

As Jack went out the door to meet his dad's car, Victoria came flying down the stairs and made a beeline for Emmy. "Okay, where is it?"

Emmy groaned and flung her gym bag over her shoulder. The bus was about to leave for the football tournament. She didn't have any time for drama. "Where is what?"

"Where is the locket my mum sent me from Paris? I know you've taken it, now hand it over!"

"I've never even seen it," Emmy said.

"You nasty little liar. You tell me where it is!"

"Oh, come on, not today." Lola stormed down the staircase. "Just ignore her, Emmy. We've got to get going."

Victoria threw her body in front of the door. "You're not going anywhere until you give me my locket!"

"She already told you, she didn't take it, so shove off!"

The door to Madam Boyd's study flew open.

"Oh, great, now you've done it," Lola muttered.

"What on God's green earth is going on out here?" Madam Boyd said.

Victoria pointed a bony finger at Emmy. "She's a thief! She stole my locket, and she's pretending not to know anything about it."

"That is a very serious accusation." Madam Boyd turned to Emmy.

"I don't know anything about her locket. I've never even seen it, so how could I have taken it?"

"I see. And what proof do you have of your accusation, Miss Stuart-Bevington?"

"It was on my dresser last night, and now it's not there."

Madam Boyd pursed her lips. "Is that all?"

"What more do you need?" Victoria asked. "She's the only person who's been in our room since I took it off last night. She would have had plenty of time to take it while I was at yoga this morning."

"I left before you did! I had an early breakfast, because I need to get on the bus with the rest of the team!"

"And they're probably waiting for us by now," Lola said.

"All right, let's hurry this along," Madam Boyd said. "Miss

Stuart-Bevington, I am sure the loss of such an item is difficult for you, but there is no proof that Miss Willick took it."

"But—"

"Anyone could have entered your room while you were both out this morning, not to mention the possibility that it may have slipped behind the dresser or been misplaced."

"I didn't—"

"I suggest you do a thorough search of your room today. I believe the rest of you have a bus to catch."

Victoria grudgingly moved out of the way and Emmy and Lola hurried to the waiting bus.

The bumpy bus ride wreaked havoc with Emmy's stomach. Why did she have so much breakfast? Why had she joined this team? What made her think she could play soccer with the kinds of teams they would be facing today? These were the best teams in southeast England. She should have just stayed home and done something productive, like doing homework or eating chocolate.

An hour later, she was standing on the sidelines, listening to "God Save the Queen," the British national anthem. Her mouth was so dry she couldn't have sung even if she had known the words. The school banner Manuela was carrying made Emmy's heart flutter more than the flag did. She'd barely seen any of Britain since she'd been here. She couldn't summon up a lot of loyalty to the flag. But Wellsworth… That was real. That was home. That was something she could be proud to represent.

The song ended, and the crowd cheered. Emmy's knees started to quake. She jumped up and down a few times and slapped her legs. She *had* to get ahold of herself. She took her position and waited.

Then the whistle blew.

The crowd roared, sending a rush of heat and energy through her veins. This was where she was meant to be. Whatever plots the Order might have, whatever happened at Latin Society, none of it mattered as long as she was on this pitch. For a fleeting moment, Emmy wondered if her father had felt this way before a rugby match. Then the ball came toward her, and she forgot all about him.

The first two matches were easy wins, but the third was tough. The Whitaker team was scrappy, and they had risen to Wellsworth's level today. Finally, Mariam scored the winning goal in the last ten minutes of play. The final match was what everyone had expected: Wellsworth versus Saint Mary's.

An official ushered the teams to the largest pitch, where the match would take place under the big stadium lights. The crowds had gotten bigger throughout the day, and by now, the stands were overflowing.

Emmy gulped. There sure were a lot of people wearing Saint Mary's blue.

Lola took a swig of water and handed Emmy a fresh bottle. "Remember, their keeper has got a weak left side. She's pretty good at reading the ball off your foot, though. So wait until the last moment to set up your shot."

"Okay."

"Stay away from the keeper's right," Lola said. "You'll never beat her there."

"Right."

"And stay away from their defenders, because they'll bash your ankles without the officials ever seeing a thing."

Within five minutes of the first whistle, it was obvious that Lola hadn't been exaggerating. The Saint Mary's side was rough. Natalie's ankle was already swelling like a softball, but she didn't want to use up a substitution to get it checked out. Ten minutes later, Dillon took an elbow to the face, but it was behind the play and the official didn't see it. By halftime, most of the team was battered and bruised, but they had managed to keep the Saint Mary's forwards in check. The score was nil–nil.

"Better keep an eye out," Lola warned Emmy. "You've

had the best chances so far, so they're going to make you their target now."

Lola was right. Every time she touched the ball, Emmy was swarmed by two or sometimes three people. But the Wellsworth defenders were just as solid, and when they headed into stoppage time, there was still no score.

Emmy was running slower and breathing harder now, and she wasn't the only one. Both teams kept turning the ball over, but no one seemed to be able to get it out of the midfield.

Finally, Lola got past her defender and moved the ball up the pitch. Emmy sprang forward. It might be their last chance before extra time. She moved into the box and made sure she knew where the last defender was. *Stay onside, Emmy. You've got to stay onside.*

Lola kicked the ball forward and Emmy ran to meet it, reached back, and—

WHAM!

She hit the ground hard and clutched her knee. It felt like someone had bashed it with a two-by-four. She looked up and saw a Saint Mary's defender looking down at her with a smug grin.

"Whoops!" the girl said.

Emmy's eyes were watering. She'd never been kicked that

hard before. She looked around for the official. This had to be worth a foul.

Finally, the official came over. "You all right?"

Emmy nodded.

"Good," she said curtly. Then she reached into her pocket, pulled out a yellow card, and pointed to the goal. Emmy glared at the Saint Mary's defender and smirked. She was going to get a penalty shot.

Emmy rubbed her aching knee. She had to numb the pain, or she wouldn't even be able to get up, let alone get off a decent shot. Finally, she stood up and took a few painful steps. It was agony. But there was no way she was going to let the Saint Mary's keeper know that.

She had to tune it all out: her teammates' screams, the crowd's cheers, and the pulsing pain in her knee.

She stared at the keeper. *Weak left side, but she knows it. That's where she'll expect me to go.*

The official had placed the ball. It was now or never.

She took a deep breath and attacked. She reached back with her right foot, bent her throbbing knee, and kicked. The ball rolled up her toes and curled right. The keeper dove left, and a moment later, the ball was in the back of the net.

The common room was boisterous that night. Madam Boyd had left early—she couldn't exactly approve of their partying, but she didn't seem too interested in stopping it. Even Victoria was in a good mood, and Emmy couldn't help but notice the gold chain dangling from her neck.

"I see you found your locket," she said.

"Eventually, though I did have to put a lot of effort into looking for it."

"Where was it?"

"Behind the dresser, and don't bother gloating about it. I'm still not convinced you didn't put it there."

Emmy rolled her eyes and took another swig of ginger ale.

A few hours later, the party was still in full swing, but Emmy could barely keep her eyes open. "I'm going to bed."

"You can't go yet," Natalie protested.

"Yeah," Jaya said, "you're the American who won the game. It's not even that late!"

"Seriously guys, I'm beat."

"But I haven't even pulled up my karaoke app yet!" Cadel said as he madly tapped away on his phone.

Lola gripped Emmy's arm. "You cannot leave me alone

down here if Cadel's going to use that app again. Last time he started singing reggae—badly."

The other team members begged Emmy to stay, but she was exhausted. She trudged up the stairs, opened the door to her room, and gasped.

It looked like a tornado had ripped through her half of the room. Everything had been dumped out of her suitcases. The mattress had been pulled off the bed, and her bedspread and pillows slashed open, the stuffing littering the floor. Her textbooks were scattered around the room, and some had their pages ripped out of the bindings. Even the pockets of her jeans and blazers had been torn out. Someone had been looking for something…and they were really angry when they did it.

A pulse started beating in Emmy's temples. *Victoria*. Who else would do something like this? Who else would destroy her things out of spite?

Emmy slammed her hand against the door and ran down the stairs. Something had finally snapped. She kept running until she reached Victoria and shoved her so hard she fell back onto the couch. "What is wrong with you? What kind of person would do that over a stupid locket?"

The common room went silent, and Victoria stared at Emmy like she had turned into Sasquatch. "Are you completely mental?"

"*ME?* You're the one who's lost her mind!"

"I don't even know what you're talking about!" Victoria shouted.

Emmy put her hands on her hips. "Yeah right, I guess my stuff just trashed itself then!"

Victoria's jaw dropped, but Emmy just shook her head. Victoria could pretend all she wanted, but Emmy knew what she had done.

People started muttering to each other. Victoria pushed past Emmy and raced up the stairs. Most of the girls followed after her, and even some of the boys went up to see the damage for themselves.

Lola passed Victoria on the stairs and reached the room first. She looked inside and swore. Victoria raced in after her and put a shaky hand to her mouth.

"Come on," Emmy scoffed, "your stuff's fine. Of course, it's fine, you're the one who did this!"

Victoria looked straight at Emmy. "I didn't do any of this."

"Oh, really? You're the one who was complaining about how much 'effort' it took to find your locket!"

"I was talking about the effort it took to move the dresser!" Victoria protested.

"I know it was you, so don't even bother trying to weasel out of this one!"

"All right, that's enough!" Lola pushed Emmy and Victoria away from each other and stood in between them. "It's a good thing my mum's already gone back to the teacher dorms or you'd both be in for it by now! We're not going to figure this out tonight, so everyone should just get to bed."

"I don't have a bed!" Emmy said.

"Arabella went home for the weekend, so you can sleep in my room," Lola said.

"But—"

Lola pressed her hand on Emmy's shoulder. "Emmy, let's just leave it for now." She was talking quietly now, and her voice was serious, almost urgent. "Come on, let's just go to bed."

Half an hour later, Emmy pulled on a pair of Lola's pajamas and yanked the covers off Arabella's bed. "I don't know why she's bothering to deny it."

"I don't know," Lola said. "That's pretty extreme...even for Victoria."

"But we know she was looking for that stupid locket today, and the person who ransacked my room was definitely looking for something. And her stuff was totally fine—not a single one of her things was out of place."

"I know, but Victoria never does anything that could actually get her into trouble. Besides, doing that much damage to your stuff would have been hard work. That's not exactly Victoria's style."

"But who else could it have been?"

Lola sat down on her own bed and drummed her fingers on her pillow. "I keep thinking about what my mum told us. About keeping your dad a secret."

"What about it?"

Lola shifted uneasily. "You said Brynn was there when you told Jonas about your dad."

"Yeah."

"It takes a lot to put my mum off, and she was really rattled when she found out who your dad was. If she's nervous about people finding out about him, there has to be a really good reason."

"You think someone from the Order ransacked my room?"

"Victoria's just not that good an actress," Lola said. "She was completely shocked when she saw your stuff. I really don't think it was her. And it's like you said: Who else could it have been?"

Emmy put her head on Arabella's pillow and pulled the covers up to her chin. "What do you think they were looking for?" she asked, even though she already knew the answer.

Lola paused. "I think it's a good thing Jack had your dad's box today."

CHAPTER 17

Staying or Going

Emmy rubbed her eyes. Why did her blanket smell funny? Like perfume and old nail polish. She looked at the comforter and groaned. Right. She was in Arabella's bed. Because her bed was trashed. She got dressed and walked to her room, where she found Lola and Madam Boyd sitting on her overturned mattress.

"When did you discover this had happened?" Madam Boyd didn't bother with any pleasantries this morning.

"Last night, when I was going to bed. I thought it was Victoria, she was looking for that stupid locket—"

"And had you been in your room since you got back from the tournament?" Madam Boyd interrupted.

"Yeah, I threw my bag in here right after I got back."

"And obviously you would have noticed if your room had been in this state then," Madam Boyd said.

Emmy's heart sank. She *would* have noticed.

"Then it couldn't have been Victoria," Lola said. "She was downstairs all evening."

Madam Boyd put her hand on Emmy's shoulder. "I'm sorry, Emmy, but this is way beyond a roommate's revenge. Someone is targeting you for something serious. I will do everything I can to find out who it is, but in the meantime, I think we need to send you home."

Madam Boyd may as well have kicked Emmy in the gut. *Send you home.* Just the thought of being sent home knocked the wind out of her.

"I don't think this was a random incident, and I am genuinely concerned for your safety," Madam Boyd said.

"You can't punish her when she hasn't done anything wrong," Lola said.

"She's not being punished, she's being protected. I don't

like it, either, but I have to put her safety above everything else."

"But—"

"I'm going to speak to the headmaster about what is to be done." Madam Boyd picked up her cane and left the room.

Emmy kicked Victoria's chair. This was completely unfair. Whatever Madam Boyd said, being sent home was definitely a punishment, and she hadn't even done anything wrong.

"I told her because I thought she might be able to help." Lola usually looked like a bull ready to charge ahead with her next great plan. Now, she looked like a helpless puppy who didn't know how to find her way home. "I didn't think she'd try and send you away."

"Just forget it," Emmy mumbled. Madam Boyd would have found out eventually. Most of Audrey House and half of Edmund House had seen her trashed room the night before. There was still stuff everywhere, and it was making Emmy claustrophobic. She unfastened the window latch and pushed the glass wide open. Droplets of rain splashed off the window frame, bouncing and tapping at her fingers.

She breathed in the familiar smell of wet pine trees and salty sea air. The forest, the mudflats, the football pitch, the common room… They all *meant* something to her now. When had she started thinking of Wellsworth as home? How could she be so rooted in a place she'd lived for less than a year? No place had ever really felt like home in Connecticut, and she'd lived there all her life.

She leaned her head against the thick wooden window frame. Jonas had said this would happen. He said eventually this place would be in her blood, just like it was in his. Her lip started wobbling. She couldn't let this happen. She couldn't leave, not now.

Lola pressed her lips together and slapped Emmy on the shoulder. "We won't let her send you away, and that's all there is to it."

"Does it really matter that much to you if I'm here?"

Lola crossed her arms and looked at the floor. "Of course it does. Let's face it, most girls can't stand me."

Emmy giggled. "They don't like me much, either. I guess we're stuck with each other."

Lola's mouth twitched. "I guess so. Besides, I don't want our team to have to find another striker."

Madam Boyd had been gone all morning, and Emmy was sitting on a couch beside Lola…waiting.

"She can't send you away," Lola said for the hundredth time. "She just can't."

Emmy shrugged. If the headmaster agreed with Madam Boyd, she was out of here and that was that.

The common room door opened, and Madam Boyd strode in. "In my office, Miss Willick." She looked annoyed. Was that a good sign or a bad sign? Maybe the headmaster was refusing to send Emmy home. Or maybe Madam Boyd had found out who had ransacked her room, and it was all some stupid prank.

"Sit down," Madam Boyd said.

Emmy closed the office door and sat in a hard chair. She slipped her hands under her knees.

"I've spoken to the headmaster and to your mother," Madam Boyd said.

Emmy pressed her lips together to stop herself from groaning. Getting her mom involved was the last thing she wanted.

"We all agree this is a very concerning incident. However, the headmaster doesn't believe this is a matter of personal safety for you."

Emmy took in a sharp breath. Did that mean what she thought it meant?

"He thinks the search was so thorough that there would be no point in anyone returning to your room."

"So, I can stay?" Emmy asked.

Madam Boyd tapped her fingers on the desk. "He didn't have all the facts, Emmy. I didn't feel it was…appropriate to discuss your father or his history here."

Emmy folded her arms across her chest. Madam Boyd could at least tell *her* about her father's history. It wasn't fair.

"I can't make you leave. I'm going to ask you to make that choice for yourself. I beg you to consider the risks and—"

"I've already considered them. I'm staying."

Madam Boyd nodded and stood up. "If that's your decision, I won't stand in your way." She opened the door. "I—"

Lola tumbled into the room, and Emmy snickered. Lola wasn't the subtlest eavesdropper. She struggled to her feet, and Madam Boyd snapped the door shut behind her.

"As you must already be aware, Miss Willick is choosing to stay at Wellsworth."

Lola gave Emmy a thumbs-up sign.

"Which means I need a promise from both of you," Madam Boyd said. "You will not be snooping into things that do not concern you. You will not be wandering at night. You will not be antagonizing others. Is that understood?" She fixed each of them with a tight stare.

They both nodded.

Madam Boyd looked straight at Lola. "And the part about not antagonizing people goes double for you."

By the time Emmy got back to her ransacked room, she had three missed phone calls from her mother. It took a long time to convince her mom that everything was okay. She told her it was just a prank, that someone was just messing around. Emmy wished she could believe that herself.

Jonas came by to ask Emmy a few questions about her ransacked room. Then Emmy and Lola started the cleanup. It took all day to get the room livable again. Jaya gave Emmy her spare bedspread, and Natalie, who was about the same size as Emmy, lent her some jeans. By the end of the weekend, her room looked almost normal again.

The next morning, Jack didn't turn up at breakfast, even though he should have gotten back the night before. At lunchtime, he ran into the Hall, grabbed a few apples, then ran back out without saying a word. They didn't see him again until humanities class, when he slid through the library door just as the last bell rang.

"Where have you been all day?" Lola demanded. "Didn't you get back last night?"

Jack glanced at Brynn and shook his head. "Later."

"All right, everyone. Let's get started," Master Barlowe called out. "Since we're meeting in the library again, I suggest you use this time to do some research for your essays on how the laws of Elizabeth I are reflected in the writings of Shakespeare. You should all be finishing your outlines and compiling your notes. If, for some inexplicable reason, you have not yet chosen your play,"—he looked straight at Lola—"I would suggest you do that now."

Everyone started getting out their books.

"Haven't you picked one yet?" Emmy rooted in her bag for her copy of *The Merchant of Venice*.

"Nah," Lola said, "I've already read them all, so it's not like it'll be hard."

Emmy shook her head. "I started it a week ago and you'll still get a better mark than me."

Jack stood up and put his bag over his shoulder. "I'm going to do some research upstairs," he said loudly.

"Uh, okay," Lola said, "knock yourself out."

Jack got a pen out of his bag, dropped it between Lola and Emmy, then reached down to pick it up. "Meet me on the third floor in five minutes," he whispered.

Before they could say anything, Jack had spun around and was sauntering up one of the iron staircases.

Emmy glanced at Lola. "What was that about?"

"Beats me."

Five minutes later, Emmy and Lola packed up their things and headed upstairs. It took a few minutes to find Jack. He was sitting in the middle of a row of books with a copy of *The Complete Works of William Shakespeare* on his lap.

"All this paranoia better be about more than *Macbeth*," Lola grumbled.

Jack put the heavy book on the floor. "Are you sure nobody followed you?"

Lola rolled her eyes, but Emmy nodded. "I'm sure."

"I heard about what happened on the weekend." Jack looked at Emmy. "Are you okay?"

Emmy tried to smile. "No harm done. So, what did you find out?"

Jack unzipped his schoolbag. "I'll tell you one thing: this box is old." He pulled out Emmy's box and handed it to her. "I looked through one of my dad's books on identifying symbols, and I found a bunch of the ones that are stamped into the box. They're all associated with Catholic Resistance groups from the sixteenth and seventeenth centuries.

"And I don't think the medallions are just for decoration. These things are solid pewter, and they're incredibly intricate. They would have been really expensive to make. There has to be a point to them, some kind of purpose."

"You think these medallions actually do something?" Emmy asked.

"I don't know," Jack said. "But look at all the grooves and holes in them. Everything looks deliberately carved."

Lola picked one up and squinted at it. "It's almost like something's missing."

"Missing?" Emmy asked.

"Yeah," Lola said. She held the medallion up to the light. "Look at these ridges. Doesn't it look like something should fit in there?"

"Maybe," Emmy said. She took the medallion and ran her fingers over it. It did feel like there was some kind of missing piece that would fit onto the back side. But what could it be? She put the medallion back in the box and closed the lid. "Listen, where do you think I should keep this box? After what happened this weekend, I don't know if my room is the best place anymore."

"You think this is what they were after?" Jack asked.

Emmy didn't say anything. She *did* think they were after the box, but she didn't want to say it out loud.

Lola started chewing on her finger nail. "There's something else I've been wondering about. Where do you think your dad got this box?"

Emmy shrugged. "How should I know?"

"It's just…" Lola looked away. It wasn't like her to beat around the bush. It made Emmy nervous.

"Do you think maybe he…stole it?"

Emmy stared at her. "Why would you think that?"

"Look, just hear me out," Lola said. "Jonas said your dad had gotten into trouble here, and—"

"He said he was a troublemaker," Emmy corrected her, "that's not the same thing."

"Yeah, well my mum's reaction to hearing his name suggests it was some pretty significant trouble."

Emmy felt her face get hot. Even though she couldn't remember her dad, it was still irritating to hear someone talk about him like that. "So, what?"

"So, somebody went to a lot of trouble to look for something in your room. It must be something incredibly valuable to whoever it was. If your dad *did* steal something from that person, it obviously hasn't been found yet."

"Maybe Emmy *should* keep the box in her room, then," Jack said.

Lola cocked her head at Jack. "Really?"

"It's like you said, they already turned her room upside down. They probably figure you don't have what they want."

"I hope you're right," Emmy said. "I don't want to buy Jaya a new bedspread." She opened her bag and put the box inside. "I think maybe I'll put the medallions in a different box, though, just to be on the safe side. Do you think…"

Suddenly she stopped. The floor was creaking nearby. Someone was in the next aisle. Emmy held her bag tight as the footsteps came closer and closer.

"Finding a lot of pertinent information, are we?" asked a cheerful voice.

Emmy breathed a sigh of relief. It was just Master Barlowe.

"Yeah, loads," Lola said.

Barlowe raised his eyebrows. "In the zoology section?"

"That's right," Lola said. "There used to be a menagerie in the Tower of London, and I needed to check something about medieval chimps."

Barlowe seemed to be trying not to laugh. "I see, and has that helped you to finally choose a play?"

"It has, actually," Lola said. "I'm going to do *The Taming of the Shrew*."

"Excellent," Barlowe said, "I suggest you get to it, then."

They hurried to the nearest staircase and Jack flicked Lola on the shoulder. "Medieval chimps? That's the best you could come up with?"

"Hey, I didn't hear you coming up with any ideas."

They reached the main floor, but Emmy stopped on the last step. She felt like she was being watched. She looked back and saw Master Barlowe looking at them from the top of the iron staircase. He smiled at her, then turned around and disappeared into the stacks.

CHAPTER 18

Easter

A lot more people stuck around for Easter break than there had been at Christmas. Jack went home, but Lola said Glasgow was too far to go to for just a few days. She and Emmy played soccer almost every day, even though the pitch was windy and wet most of the time. "That's how you know you're in the UK," Lola would say. There was always hot chocolate waiting for them in the Hall, which they usually brought back to the common room, so they could play Lola's slapping card game.

On the last day of break, Lola woke up Emmy at the crack of dawn. "It's our last day before teachers start piling on homework again. We have to spend as much time on the pitch as possible."

Emmy groaned. "I still have to finish my homework from last week."

Lola waved her hand like homework was no big deal. "Meet me downstairs in ten minutes."

Fifteen minutes later Emmy trudged down the stairs. "Do we at least get to have breakfast first?"

"If you insist." Lola handed her an envelope. "By the way, someone put this in my mailbox by mistake."

Emmy took the envelope and frowned. It was addressed to her and was the same size and shape as the one she'd found in her coat pocket on Christmas day. That couldn't be a coincidence.

Emmy fumbled with the seal and a small piece of paper fell out onto the floor. She grabbed it and read:

Sent to Thomas Allyn on October 4, 2004.

She turned it over and started to read:

Dear Tom,
The Order knows you're in America. It's only a

*matter of time before they figure out where. They
are coming. You need to run.*

Emmy started to shake. October 4, 2004. That was two
weeks before her third birthday. Two weeks before her father
had disappeared. The room started spinning. It couldn't be
true. Why would a little school society want her father dead?
This box couldn't be that valuable. It couldn't be worth
someone's life. Could it?

"Emmy, you okay?" Lola grabbed her arm. "Sit down,
you look like you're about to keel over." She led Emmy to an
armchair. "What is it?"

Emmy showed her the note, but she didn't say anything. It
felt like she'd swallowed sandpaper.

Lola looked around the room, where there were a few people
lingering before breakfast. "Let's go back to your room."

They went upstairs, and Lola locked the door behind them.
"What do you think this means?"

"It means the Order came after my dad," Emmy whispered.
"They might have even killed him." She thought about the
shoebox that hid the medallions under her bed, and the real box
she'd stuffed inside her suitcase. "And I probably have what
they're looking for, which means they might come after me, too."

Lola looked grimmer than Emmy had ever seen her. "You need to stay away from them, Em. You should stop going to Latin Society and mind your own business."

Emmy didn't say anything at first. Lola was probably right. She could even give the Order the box and be done with it. But that made her stomach churn more than the things written in that letter.

"I can't. If my dad died rather than give them that box, the minute I hand it over, it means he would have died for nothing. Living with that would be worse than living with the Order on my tail."

"ARE YOU OUT OF YOUR BLOODY MIND?" Jack shouted.

"Shh!" Emmy hissed. She glanced around the mudflats, which looked as deserted as ever. She and Lola had brought Jack here as soon as he'd gotten back to school. Emmy wanted plenty of distance between her and any Order members before she started talking about her dad.

"What else am I supposed to do?" Emmy asked.

"Stop going to Latin Society. Stop investigating the Order."

Emmy felt her face flush. "I can't!"

"But—"

"I know what you're going to say, Jack, and I don't want to hear it. I'm not going to stop learning about the Order."

"What about ringing the police?" Lola said.

"What's the point?" Emmy asked. "This letter doesn't prove anything, it doesn't even implicate anyone. What proof do I have that my dad really did get this letter two weeks before he disappeared? I need more evidence."

Jack looked like he was about to jump out of his skin. "Emmy, I really don't think you understand how serious this is. My family has been connected to the Order for generations. I've heard all the whispering about deals that have gone bad, and people getting hurt. I know what they're capable of."

"I've had to live without my dad for ten years, Jack. No one knows what they're capable of better than I do."

Jack looked away.

"I know this is dangerous, but I need to know. I'm going to find out everything I can about the Order of Black Hollow Lane, and I'm going to find out if they killed my dad."

Jack rubbed his temples. "Fine. So, what are we going to do next?"

Emmy blinked. "Uh, *we?*"

"Of course, *we*," Lola said.

Emmy shook her head. "I'm not asking you to do anything, I can do this on my own."

Lola snorted. "No offense, Emmy, but you need us."

"No way," Emmy said, "I'm not going to put you guys in danger."

"Sorry," Jack said, "but you don't get to decide this part. It'll be much safer if we stick together. Safety in numbers and all that, right?"

"Right, like the Three Musketeers," Lola said. "One for all—"

"—and all for one," Jack finished.

A few days later, Emmy was running to Latin Society, holding her jacket over her head to keep out a torrential downpour of rain.

She finally made it to the little cottage, reached around the spiky plant, and pushed the skull; the wall opened.

"Ah, Emmeline!" Master Larraby called. "So good to see you, my dear!"

Emmy stared at him. Master Larraby never spoke to her at Latin Society, not unless she asked him a specific question about her homework.

"Why don't you join me by the fire?"

Emmy glanced around the room. Some of the boys were looking at her. Maybe they were wondering why Larraby was talking to her. She was wondering, too. She followed Larraby to a plush leather sofa.

"Crumpet?" Larraby pointed to a plate on the coffee table.

Emmy eyed them warily. "Uh, no thanks."

Larraby grabbed one and stuffed it in his mouth. "You know," he said between mouthfuls, "I was just thinking that you and I need to get to know one another better."

Emmy raised an eyebrow.

"It's been nearly a whole school year since you joined our little club," Larraby went on, "and we barely know you. Now, you're from Massachusetts, correct?"

"Um, Connecticut."

"Of course," Larraby said. "Do they have any big cities in Connecticut?"

"I guess Bridgeport's kinda big, but—"

"And that's where you're from? Bridgeport?"

"No, I'm from Gretna. It's closer to Stamford."

"Ah yes," Larraby said. "And your parents…they both live in Gretna as well?"

Emmy shifted in her seat. "I live with my mom."

"I see, I see. Your parents are divorced then?"

"My father's dead."

"That must have been very difficult." Larraby's voice was sympathetic, but his expression was cold, almost hungry. "It's never easy, losing a parent. You must treasure all the reminders you have of him."

Emmy didn't say anything. She knew where Larraby was going with this.

"You must value any items that belonged to him above all others." Larraby looked expectantly at Emmy, but she still didn't say anything.

"Tell me, did your father…leave you anything? Anything to remember him by?"

Emmy stared straight into Larraby's eyes. "My mother destroyed all his possessions after he died."

"Destroyed?" Larraby looked shocked. "Everything he had? Correspondence…mementos…"

"She got rid of it all," Emmy said. "She didn't want any reminders of what happened."

Larraby shook his head. "I must admit, I find that hard to believe."

"You can ask her about it if you like," Emmy said. "She's traveling, but I can give you her phone number." She didn't think he'd actually get in touch with her mom, but if he did, her mom would back up her story. It was the truth. Mostly. Her mom *had* gotten rid of all her dad's things. She'd just gotten her hands on a few since then.

"So, you have nothing that belonged to him?"

Emmy's heart skipped a beat. She had to be careful with this answer. "It's like I told you, my mom destroyed everything we had of his."

Larraby's shoulders slumped. "What a pity." He stood up and walked away.

"I don't know if you should keep going," Jack said when Emmy told him and Lola what had happened "Larraby's probably going to keep asking questions. What if you let something slip? What if he figures out you really do have the box?"

"He's right." Lola leaned in close to Jack and Emmy. "Right now, he thinks there's only one place it can't be—your room at school. If that's what he's looking for, he's going to keep asking questions until he figures out where it is."

Emmy brushed a few raindrops out of her hair. "I think *he's* the one who's going to let something slip. He knows something about my dad. Why else would he be asking me all those questions about him? This is my chance to get more information."

Over the next few weeks, Larraby asked more and more questions. What did her dad do for a living? Did her house have any secret passageways or rooms? Larraby wasn't exactly subtle, and the stress of coming up with vague answers was starting to get to Emmy. She was having trouble sleeping and trouble concentrating in her classes. Larraby had to give something away eventually. Maybe she should start listening outside his office door.

She rubbed her eyes as she made her way to humanities class one day. Just a few more days. She was *sure* she was getting close to a breakthrough. She just had to hang on a few more days and Larraby would crack.

When she got to the humanities classroom, Jack and Lola were standing outside with most of the rest of the class.

"Door's locked," Lola said.

Jack looked at his watch. "Barlowe must be running late."

"Finally learned to tell time, Jacklyn?" someone sneered. Emmy stiffened. Brynn was walking toward them. "When we were roommates, you couldn't even tie your shoelaces."

Jack looked away.

"Just ignore him," Lola said loudly.

"Oh, that's right," Brynn said, his eyes glinting. "I forgot you hired a guard dog."

Victoria giggled, and Lola said something to Brynn that she probably wouldn't have if her mom had been around.

"Temper, temper, dear cousin. I guess you get your manners from your mother. No wonder Granddad cut you two off. I guess every family has an unstable element that needs to be pruned so it doesn't kill the family tree. Thank goodness we got rid of your mum when we did   otherwise she might have contaminated us."

Lola launched herself at Brynn, but Emmy and Jack grabbed onto her shoulders and held her back.

"He's not worth it, Lola," Jack said as he struggled to hold on to her. "Just let it go."

"Yeah, he's just trying to get you expelled," Emmy said. "It's pathetic."

"And now the redhead joins the fray," Brynn said.

"Uh oh," Victoria said with a grin, "careful, Emmeline. Isn't your mummy a parenting expert? She wouldn't want you to say anything that might embarrass her."

"Where did you get that red hair?" Brynn asked. "Must be from that deadbeat dad of yours. What a loser, no wonder your mum's ashamed of him."

It happened in the blink of an eye: Emmy let go of Lola, reached back, and punched Brynn square in the face. He doubled over, his hand over his eye, moaning like a wounded animal.

"Shut up!" She lunged for Brynn again. Jack and Lola pulled her back, and she struggled to yank herself free. Something inside her had snapped.

"Miss Willick!" shouted someone from the end of the corridor. Emmy's heart sank. Master Barlowe had arrived.

"What on earth is going on here?" he asked, walking quickly through the crowd of students.

Emmy stopped struggling. Anger was still burning in her stomach, but other emotions were starting to creep in. Shock. Panic. Remorse. She had just punched someone. In the face.

"Well?" Barlowe asked.

Emmy opened her mouth, but no sound came out. Her tongue felt like lead.

"She attacked me for no reason, sir," Brynn croaked, still holding his eye.

Master Barlowe glared at Brynn. "I doubt it was for no reason, Mr. Stratton, but nothing excuses physical violence in a school corridor." Barlowe unlocked the door. "Do you need to see a nurse?"

Brynn glowered at Emmy, then shook his head.

"Very well," Barlowe said, "everyone come inside. Miss Willick, we'll talk about this after class."

Emmy nodded and walked numbly into the room. Victoria looked almost as shocked as Emmy felt. Her face was beet red, and she kept looking down and readjusting her ponytail. She found a seat far away from Emmy and didn't look at her for the rest of the day.

Barlowe broke everyone into groups to discuss the ethical issues involved in the imprisonment of Mary, Queen of Scots, but Emmy didn't hear a word of what her group said. Not that anyone in class was talking about Mary, Queen of Scots. The little snippets Emmy heard were all about her, Brynn, and his ever-blackening eye. Even Master Barlowe seemed distracted. He usually patrolled the groups and joined in on discussions, but he just sat at his desk and stared at the wall. When the bell rang, everyone bolted for the door. Everyone except Emmy.

She couldn't stop tucking her hair behind her ear. Her mouth was as dry as sand, and her hand was killing her. Who knew punching someone could hurt the person doing the punching?

A minute passed, and Master Barlowe was still sitting at his desk, staring into space. Was Emmy supposed to speak first?

What was she supposed to say? She seemed to have developed a sudden case of laryngitis.

Finally, Barlowe looked at her. "Where did that come from, Emmy?"

"I'm sorry, sir," she blurted, "I don't... I don't know what happened. He said something... I know it's no excuse, but—"

"You're right, it's not," Barlowe interrupted. "I'm sure I don't need to tell you that violence solves nothing. It only leads to more violence."

Emmy nodded.

Barlowe folded his hands and pressed his fingers to his lips. "I've never known you to be an angry person, Emmy. And even though there's no excuse, it must have been something serious to cause you to react that way." He stared at Emmy, and she bit her lip. He didn't look angry. He looked worried.

The knot in Emmy's stomach unclenched a little. "He said something about my dad. About him being a deadbeat, and my mom being ashamed of him."

Barlowe cleared his throat. "I see. It sounds like your father is a...a sensitive topic for you."

Emmy was silent. The Order might have killed her dad. Then again, he might have left to escape them. So why hadn't he taken his family along? Why hadn't he come back? Did she mean anything to him at all? The fact of the matter was, Brynn hadn't said anything she hadn't thought herself.

"I had a challenging relationship with my father," Barlowe said. "If you ever feel the need to speak to anyone about your dad…" He broke off, still looking at Emmy.

She twisted her fingers together. It would be nice to talk to someone who understood. But Madam Boyd's voice still rang in her ears: *tell no one.*

"Thanks," she said, "but I'm fine. I'm sorry about Brynn… I know I shouldn't have hit him."

Master Barlowe's face fell. He seemed disappointed she hadn't confided in him. "I cannot allow physical violence to go unpunished, even if Mr. Stratton deserved it. You can wash some of the walls in the humanities wing as your detention. Come by around seven tomorrow night."

"Yes, sir." Emmy grabbed her bag and was about to open the door when she looked back. "Master Barlowe?"

"Yes?"

"Thank you, sir." There were times when she didn't know what to make of Barlowe. He acted strangely sometimes, like when he didn't seem happy about the extra work they'd done on their cathedral assignment, but he was also kind and helpful. He genuinely seemed to care. Maybe the odd things he did were just part of his quirky charm. Emmy smiled at him. She wanted him to know how much she appreciated everything.

She left the classroom and hurried back to the common room, where she found Jack and Lola waiting.

"Well?" Jack asked.

"Detention," Emmy answered. "I have to wash the walls in the hallway tomorrow night."

Lola gaped at her. "That's it? Wash a few bleeding walls? I worked in the library for three months after I slugged him!"

"You did break his nose," Jack reminded her. "Not to mention your list of prior offenses."

"It's not my fault he has a delicate little nose. Next time I'll aim for his eye like Emmy did."

Emmy stayed in the common room for a long time that night. She'd hoped Victoria would be fast asleep by the time she went to her room, but Victoria was sitting up in bed, reading a magazine in the lamplight.

Emmy slipped off her shoes and started rifling for her pajamas.

"Well, that was unexpected." Victoria flipped a page of her magazine. "I didn't really think you were the punching type."

Emmy kicked off her jeans. "What are you going to do? Call my 'mummy the parenting expert' and tattle on me?"

"I would have thought you'd already talked to her. If I had a parenting expert for a mum, I'd tell her everything."

"So, I could see my life used as an example in her next book? No, thanks."

Victoria slammed her magazine shut. "At least your mum is actually interested in your life." She flicked off her lamp and threw her head on the pillow, rustling the covers up to her chin.

Emmy yanked her pajama shirt over her head. Victoria was completely clueless. Emmy's mom didn't even call her on her birthday, so how could anyone say she was interested in her life? Victoria's mom probably spoiled her rotten. Except, now that she thought about it, Emmy had never actually heard Victoria talk about her mom. She'd never heard them talking on the phone, and she hadn't been the one to pick Victoria up at Christmas. She didn't actually know that much about her roommate. Not that it was all Emmy's fault. Victoria had never exactly been friendly.

Emmy pulled out her phone. She *could* text her mom. But that would probably just lead to a lecture. She turned off the phone and crawled under the covers. She'd had enough hard conversations for one day.

CHAPTER 19

Detention

When Emmy came back to the humanities wing the next night, Barlowe had a sponge and soapy bucket ready for her. "The walls are looking pretty scruffy in this corridor." He pointed to the end of the hallway. "That one will be fine, nobody ever goes down there. Just get the other three and that'll be enough."

He looked at his watch. "I have to meet a student in the library, but if you're done before I get back, just leave the' bucket here and I'll get to it later." He disappeared down the corridor and Emmy started scrubbing.

It didn't take long to do the three walls that Barlowe had asked for. The ceilings were so low in this hallway that the walls weren't that big. She looked at her watch. She might as well do the wall at the end, even if she didn't have to. Barlowe had been her favorite teacher this year, and she wanted to go the extra mile.

The end wall was really dirty, which didn't make any sense. The closest classroom was twenty feet away, but this wall was covered in finger smudges. Her sponge kept getting stuck on the same stubborn spot. There were all these grooves and little pieces that stuck out, which made it impossible to clean. She sighed. She'd come back to that one later.

But there was another stubborn spot a little higher. This one felt more like a shape, like something had been stamped into the stone. She squinted at the wall and just about dropped her sponge. It was the Order's symbol. It was so worn down she could barely see it, but the skull was definitely there. She ran her fingers over it and pushed. Nothing happened.

Water dripped from her sponge and puddled on the floor. This symbol kept popping up in the strangest places. It couldn't be an accident that it was on this wall and not on the next. There had to be a reason.

"What am I missing?" She ran her fingers over the symbol, then down along the wall. There were those grooves, the ones she couldn't get clean. She frowned. They didn't feel like they'd been worn in over time. They felt intentionally hammered out. And they were right underneath the skull. They felt like an outline, as if something would fit inside them. There were smooth circles that jutted out, like they were waiting for something to complete them. It was as if something was…

"…missing," Emmy whispered.

Her heart started to race. Could this be the missing piece she'd been looking for? She threw the sponge into the bucket and ran to Audrey House, flying up the stairs without so much as a glance at anyone in the room. She burst into her room and dove under her bed. Where was it? Finally, her fingers brushed the box. She grabbed it, stuffed it into her schoolbag, and sprinted across the grounds until she reached the humanities wing.

Okay, slow down. Make sure no one's following you.

She glanced behind her and deliberately took a wrong turn. No one came after her. Quietly and carefully, she made her way back to the wall. With one last look down the empty hallway, she pulled out the shoebox and gently lifted the lid. Twelve medallions, all different shapes, all with grooves and curves that seemed deliberately hammered into place. Just like the spot on the wall.

Emmy tapped the edge of the box. The spot on the wall had three points that stuck out like nails. That meant she needed a medallion with three holes. The first one she saw only had two, and the next one didn't have any. The third one had three holes, but it was way too big.

She picked up the fourth one and rubbed its shiny surface. It looked worn around the edges, like it had been used more than the others. It had three small holes. This one might work. She placed the holes onto the points. They fit. Then she pushed on the medallion and heard a distinct *click*.

The hair on the back of her neck stood up. Something else must be about to happen.

But nothing did. No secret doorway, no hidden passage. Everything was just as it was before.

Emmy's shoulders slumped. She hadn't imagined that *click*. It sounded like an old-fashioned lock clacking into place.

Then she heard another noise, but it wasn't from the wall, it was from a nearby corridor. *Footsteps*.

She pulled the medallion off the wall and dropped it back into the box. She had just shoved the box into her bag when Master Barlowe rounded the corner. "Still here, are we?"

"I just finished." Emmy threw her bag over her shoulder. If only she'd had a few more minutes.

"Excellent." Barlowe picked up the soapy bucket and looked at where Emmy was standing. "Were you washing the far wall?"

Emmy nodded.

Barlowe frowned. "I thought I said that wasn't necessary."

"Oh, uh, it seemed pretty dirty, so I figured I may as well wash that one, too." She'd thought Barlowe would be glad that she took some initiative, but he didn't look too happy. "Sorry, I didn't realize it would be a problem."

Barlowe smiled, but his face still seemed tight. "Of course, it's no problem. You'd better get back to your house before Madam Boyd accuses me of indentured servitude."

Emmy thanked him and hurried back to Audrey House, hugging her bag to her chest.

"And you're sure you heard it click?" Jack asked.

Emmy nodded and pulled her jacket tight around her shoulders. She had dragged Jack and Lola to the mudflats again. There was no way she would risk being overheard tonight.

Lola whistled. "Unbelievable. So, did you open it?"

"Open what?" Emmy asked.

"The door," Lola said.

"There was no door," Emmy said. "Nothing happened after I heard the click."

"But the click—it sounded like a lock clacking into place?" Lola asked.

"Yeah, but—"

"So, it must have been a door, and you must have unlocked it!"

"But how do I open it?" Emmy asked.

"The same way you open any door—by turning the knob!"

Emmy stared at Lola. "But there was no knob. The only thing on the wall was the medallion."

"Exactly."

Emmy's face broke into a smile. "You think it's the key and the doorknob?"

"There's only one way to find out." Lola's eyes twinkled. She and Emmy raced up the bank and had almost reached the edge of the forest when they realized Jack wasn't with them. He was standing in the muddy valley, hands stuffed into his pockets.

"You don't have to come with us." Emmy said.

Jack kicked a muddy stone and it squelched into a nearby puddle. "No, I'll come, if that's what you decide you want to do."

"What's there to decide?" Lola asked. "There's a door, we've got to go through it."

"Maybe, if it's worth it. I just don't know if it is."

Emmy walked back down the bank. "I know it's risky but finding out about my dad *is* worth it."

"But why would there be any information about your dad on the other side of that door?" He looked at Emmy with a pleading expression, like he was desperate to get through to her. "Your dad disappeared ten years ago, and he probably hasn't had anything to do with the Order since then. What do you think you'll find?"

"I don't know, maybe some kind of proof they killed him."

"But why would they keep any kind of evidence that they're murderers?" Jack asked. "And let's say, by some miracle, you stumbled on this proof you're looking for. What then? What would that mean?"

Emmy shuffled her feet. "I just want answers. I want to know what happened to him."

"I want that for you, too, but unless there's some reason you think you'll find them behind that door, I don't know if it's worth the risk of them catching you."

Emmy twisted her toe into the sand. As much as she hated to admit it, Jack might have a point.

"All I'm asking is that you think about it. Waiting a few extra days won't make a difference. If we're going to go head-to-head against the Order, you'd better be sure."

Emmy did think about it, and for more than a few days. The end of term was getting closer, and she still hadn't decided if she would look behind the wall in the humanities wing. She didn't know what was back there, and if she stumbled on some Order members, she wouldn't stand much of a chance. It also wasn't just her neck she'd be risking—Jack and Lola insisted on coming with her, and if she was really honest with herself, she didn't know if she'd have the guts to do it without them.

She had less and less time to think about it now that exams were starting. The common room had been turned into a study zone, and everyone was feeling the pressure.

"What kind of things were on your second-year Latin exam?" Emmy asked two days before her first exam.

"Not much," Lola said. "Verbs, vocab, that sort of thing."

"Not worrying about your exam, are you Emmeline?" said

a deep voice behind them. Emmy did a double take. Even though Master Larraby was the head of Edmund House, he rarely came into their common room. "I was just coming to see how you were getting along with your studies."

Lola raised an eyebrow at Emmy. Master Larraby didn't usually put much effort into helping his students.

"Uh, I'm doing fine, I think," Emmy said.

"Splendid. Just make sure you review *Tusculan Disputations*."

Emmy stared at him. "*What?*"

"*Tusculan Disputations*. We did go over them, didn't we?"

Emmy's mouth went dry. "Um, no sir. I don't think we did."

"Oh, I'm sure we did, you must have just forgotten. Not to worry, I have a worksheet about them somewhere. How about you come by my office tomorrow at three thirty, I'll give it to you then."

Emmy nodded, and Larraby swept from the room.

"What are *Tusculan Disputations*?" Emmy asked.

"Beats me," Lola said.

"You haven't learned it yet, either?"

"No," Jack said.

Lola looked around the room. "Hey, Dillon!" A sixth-year girl from their soccer team turned around. "What are *Tusculan Disputations*?"

"Some books written by Cicero around two thousand years ago," Dillon said. "We read some of them this year."

"Just now, in sixth year?" Emmy asked.

Dillon nodded, and Emmy groaned. "Then why would I have to know them for my second-year exam?"

"He's probably just mixed up the exams," Lola said. "You know what he's like."

"Yeah, but what if he mixed it up when he was making the exam?"

"Oh relax," Lola said. "Just read through the worksheet and be done with it."

The next day, Emmy went to Larraby's office at three thirty on the dot. She raised her hand to knock, then stopped. Larraby was talking to someone.

"I know," Larraby was saying. "But don't you think that..." There was silence. "Yes, I agree." There was silence again; it sounded like Larraby was on the phone. "Things haven't gone to plan with the Allyn girl."

Emmy froze, her hand poised over the door like a statue.

"I haven't been able to get a single thing out of her," Larraby continued. "And she's far too inquisitive for her own good." There was another pause. "Thankfully she hasn't, and I don't see how she could. Heaven help us if she did."

Emmy moved closer to the door. *I haven't what?*

"We'll keep an eye out. If she ever found her way onto the Lane… No, I don't see how she could. She doesn't have a medallion, there's no way she could get in."

Emmy sucked in her breath. So, using a medallion *would* get her onto Black Hollow Lane.

"Thank goodness for that. We'd be finished if she ever found all the information we have down there about Thomas."

Emmy felt like her chest was going to explode. *Thomas.* They had information about her dad. And she knew how to get to it.

"Yes, she's on her way here now, so I'd best be off; she's annoyingly prompt."

Emmy put her hand over her mouth and closed her eyes. She had to get that worksheet, otherwise he'd be suspicious.

She took a few slow breaths, then knocked.

"Come in!" Larraby called.

Emmy opened the door and Larraby flashed her a toothy grin. "Ah, Emmeline, I'm glad you came! It'll give us a chance to chat!"

"Oh, uh, sorry, but I can't stay." Emmy twisted her fingers behind her back. "I'm, uh, meeting a study group."

"Oh, what a pity, I had hoped to spend a bit more time with you before the end of the year."

"I'm already late, so I should really just get my worksheet and go."

Larraby studied her face, probably to figure out if she'd overheard him. Emmy smiled and tried to look as relaxed as possible.

Larraby smiled back and nodded. "Of course, I won't keep you then." He handed her a worksheet. Emmy thanked him and tried to keep her excitement in check as she walked out the door. As soon as the office was out of sight, she raced back to Audrey House, her brain working with every step. *The Lane. A medallion. Thomas. Dad.*

She slowed down when she got to the edge of the forest and tried to catch her breath. If Brynn saw her agitated after meeting with Larraby, he might get suspicious.

Emmy didn't pull Jack and Lola aside until after dinner. She couldn't risk doing anything suspicious, not today. When she finally told them, Lola's eyes grew wider and wider, and Jack's frown grew deeper and deeper.

"So, what are you going to do?" he asked.

"I'm going down there," Emmy said. "And don't bother trying to talk me out of it."

She was ready for a fight with Jack, but he just shook his head. "I was just wondering whether we should stick together down there or split up so we can find it faster?"

"Together?" Emmy said. "No way, you guys shouldn't come down there... It's not safe."

"All the more reason we should come," Jack said. "It'll be faster and safer if there are more of us."

"No, I can't let you—"

"Don't be stupid," Lola said. "We're not missing this."

"Let's face it," Jack said, "you need us."

CHAPTER 20

Black Hollow Lane

Emmy lay awake, staring at the ceiling. She tried not to think about what they were going to do. Or what they might find on the other side of that wall. They were waiting until the middle of the night, hoping that there wouldn't be any Order members down there, but there was no guarantee.

When she went downstairs on the stroke of two, Jack and Lola were already waiting for her. "Are you sure you guys want to come?"

"Don't bother asking," Lola said.

Emmy looked at Jack.

"We're with you," he said.

Emmy smiled grimly and handed each of them a brown paper bag.

"What's this?" Jack asked.

"Keep them in your pockets," Emmy said. "Just in case."

Jack looked inside the bag, swallowed hard, then put it in the pocket of his hoodie.

Emmy hoisted her bag onto her shoulder. "Let's go."

"Are you sure we won't be seen by the security cameras again?" Jack asked as they made their way through the grounds.

"At two in the morning?" Lola said. "What are the chances that Jonas is still awake and looking at the cameras *again*?"

"Besides," Emmy said, "even if he did, we'd be gone by the time he got there. I'm not standing in that hallway any longer than I have to."

Slowly and carefully, they crept into the main building. The emergency lights sputtered and flickered with an eerie green glow. Emmy shivered. Those lights hadn't spooked her the last time. Then again, she hadn't been trying to sneak into the headquarters of a potentially murderous society the last time.

They tiptoed through the school and down the long flight

of stairs that led to the old humanities wing. Emmy looked over her shoulder. The whole wing seemed deserted. Finally, they reached the wall.

"Last chance to back out." She pulled a medallion out of her pocket.

"Just do it," Jack said grimly.

Emmy took a deep breath and rubbed her hand along the wall. There was the spot, exactly where she remembered it. "Here goes nothing." She fit the medallion into place.

Click.

The sound echoed off the stone walls, and Jack glanced at a nearby security camera. "Okay, try turning it."

Emmy gripped the medallion and turned.

Clack.

A breeze blew into the hallway as a wide crack opened, revealing a long set of narrow stone steps. Emmy pulled the medallion off the wall and walked onto the little landing at the top of the staircase. Jack and Lola squeezed in behind her, and Lola started feeling around on the door.

"What are you looking for?" Jack asked.

"The handle. There it is." She pulled the door shut.

"Are you sure we can get back through?" Jack asked with a wavering voice.

"It's a proper handle on this side," Lola said, "so just get going and stop being such a baby."

The steps were smooth and slippery. Dim light bulbs flickered here and there, but they didn't give off much light.

"Looks like a bloody bomb shelter," Lola muttered.

The stairs seemed to go down forever, twisting and turning and constantly changing pitch. Finally, they reached the bottom. A long stone passageway stretched out in front of them, and just like the staircase, they couldn't see how far it went.

A light bulb buzzed overhead. Nobody walked forward. It was a lot harder to be brave down here.

"How far underground do you think we are?" Emmy asked.

"Far enough that no one in the school would ever hear what goes on down here," Jack said.

Emmy took a deep breath, then started walking. They walked and walked for what felt like a mile, even though it probably wasn't. They turned a corner, and all three of them stopped in their tracks. A pale light glowed nearby, much too bright to be a light bulb.

"Do you think someone's down there?" Jack whispered.

"Only one way to find out," Emmy said.

They walked closer and closer, following the glow like

moths drawn to a porch light. Emmy squinted. Where was that light coming from? "I think I can see an archway."

The light was bright enough to see each other's faces. Lola was white as a sheet, and Jack looked ready to throw up.

"Anyone want to turn back?" Emmy half hoped they'd say yes.

They both shook their heads, but not as firmly as when she'd asked the same question earlier. Finally, they reached the archway and walked through.

They were in a large round room. The glow was coming from a huge lantern that hung from an archway in the middle, almost like a small stone gazebo. Above the lantern there was a carving that read, "Hollingworth Square."

"Now what?" Jack asked.

"There must be some kind of office," Emmy said, "or a file room that has the info about my dad. We need to find it."

Lola checked her watch. "We'd better hurry. We can't risk anyone seeing us on the cameras or running into us when we get back up to the school."

Emmy looked at all the corridors that led to who-knows-where. It was so much bigger than she'd imagined. She should have planned for more time. "We need to split up. We'll cover more ground, and there's no way there's anybody down here now."

Lola looked at Jack. "What do you think?"

Jack cleared his throat and nodded. "We don't have much choice. I don't want to have to try this again."

"Okay, but we should meet back here every fifteen minutes to make sure we don't get lost," Emmy said.

"Agreed," Jack said. He walked to the closest archway and ran his hands through his hair. "Good luck."

"I don't believe in luck," Lola said, and she disappeared down another corridor.

Emmy looked at her watch to make sure she knew when to be back, then went through the archway straight across from the one they'd come in. She'd only gone twenty feet when she saw another tunnel on her left. Should she take it? No. She'd better keep going straight if she was going to figure out how to get back.

"Should have brought a compass," she muttered.

Every few minutes, she passed another doorway. She looked at her watch and started to walk faster; she was going to have to turn back soon. The ceilings started getting taller, and the light bulbs were replaced with lanterns that hung from iron hooks. She must be getting into an older part of the tunnels. Then she froze. The lanterns were lit. That meant someone must have lit them.

She turned around and started to run. She needed to get back to Jack and Lola; they should never have split up. Suddenly, one of the corridor's walls moved. It scraped along the floor and banged into the next wall, like a door slamming shut. A hooded figure stood with his body pressed against it. He had blocked the hallway, so she couldn't get through.

"That's better," the figure said. "We should be far enough away now that your friends won't hear us." He turned toward Emmy. She squinted, but the hallway was so dark, and his hood fell so low that she couldn't see his face.

"I'm sorry it's come to this," he said, "but you have something of mine, and I need it back now." He stepped into the lantern light.

Emmy's mouth went dry. No. It couldn't be.

He pulled back his hood. "Welcome to Black Hollow Lane, young miss." It was Jonas.

CHAPTER 21

The Round Tower

Emmy couldn't speak. She couldn't move. She couldn't do anything but stare.

"This wasn't how I wanted things to happen," Jonas said, "but sometimes I have to make tough choices as Brother Loyola."

"You're Brother Loyola?"

"At the moment, yes. There was another Brother Loyola before me, and there will be another one after. There will always be a Brother Loyola to look after the Order of Black Hollow Lane."

"But I thought… Larraby…"

"Yes, Larraby does have his uses. All his blundering makes him an excellent decoy, and he does like to feel involved. When I had him stage that phone call for you to overhear, I wasn't sure he'd be able to pull it off. But I had to get you down here, and I had no other options left."

The phone call in Larraby's office. It was fake, and it wasn't the only thing. Jonas's kindness… All his helpful suggestions. It was all fake. She wanted to scream at him. She wanted to burst into tears. But she had to keep her head. He wasn't her friend Jonas anymore. He was Brother Loyola, and he was blocking the only way she knew how to get out of here.

Get him talking. Give yourself time to think.

"Why did you need to get me down here?"

"I saw you in the humanities wing that night. I know you have a medallion."

Emmy's insides lurched. "You were watching me?"

"I've been keeping a close eye on you for a while. Ever since you asked me about Tom."

Hot sweat prickled at the back of Emmy's neck. How could she have been so stupid that she'd told Jonas about her dad? Why had she even brought him up? Jonas… He'd said he'd found her gloves at the church…but she thought he was returning something else. "My letter. You knew Brynn had my dad's letter."

Jonas nodded. "Mr. Stratton can be a bit…direct when he wants information. Sometimes he needs a little reining in. But it was the first link we'd had to Tom in years. I couldn't let him be punished for it."

Of course. Jonas was the one who had told Brynn about them breaking into the office. She should have figured that out ages ago.

"Finding out Thomas Allyn was your father changed everything."

"Why?"

"I told you I knew Tom, and I did. At least, I thought I did. He was my roommate."

Emmy's fingers twitched. She should be figuring out how to get out of here. But her dad's roommate was standing in front of her, and she couldn't get her feet to move. She wanted— *needed*—to hear his story.

"Tom and I were recruited by the Order in our fifth year at Wellsworth. We rose quickly through the ranks, and by the time we left school, we were part of Brother Loyola's inner circle of advisers. When we left school, we were both given tasks. I was in charge of recruitment, and Tom was in charge of establishing a political presence in London."

"A political presence? Like some kind of party, like the Democrats or the Republicans?"

"The Order doesn't answer to any particular political stripe. Our only goal is to look after our own. Each member plays a part in ensuring that the Order as a whole has as much influence as possible."

"I don't get it."

"Why should we form a political party when that would mean our only influence is in politics? Our members include scientists, diplomats, prime ministers, Nobel laureates. We work together to ensure each member gets the life he deserves. Let's say one member sees another's name on a list for a possible promotion. He makes sure that promotion happens. Or maybe a member owns an oil company and he wants permission to drill in the North Sea. We'll have someone placed in government who can ensure permission goes ahead. Right now, I'm helping a young man develop his skills in recruitment. He comes to Wellsworth every once in a while, and I mentor him as he works with our boys. All of us benefit."

He comes to Wellsworth every once in a while... He

works with our boys... "Vincent!" Emmy said. "You're still mentoring Vincent Galt, aren't you? That's why he's been hanging around the school."

Jonas nodded. "One member helps another, and our influence grows."

Emmy frowned. That didn't sound so bad. "Why would the Order have gone after my dad if it was just a club where members help each other? That doesn't sound like something worth killing someone over."

"As our influence has grown, it has needed to move outside the law. Dealing in weapons, the black market, the underground diamond trade—these are all necessary parts of our work."

A nasty feeling slithered up Emmy's throat. The Order sounded like some kind of mafia. Jonas was talking about "influence." That was just another word for power.

Barlowe had said something about power when they visited the round-tower church.

There will always be people who crave power. And people who will go to any lengths to hold on to it.

An icy tingle twitched at Emmy's spine. What lengths would Jonas go to?

He started pacing, his feet scuffing the old stone floor. "I thought Tom and I were on the same page. I thought he believed in our mission. But in our last year of school, he started having second thoughts. One of his friends was injured when an initiation ritual went too far. The girl was in the wrong place at the wrong time. It was just an accident. I kept his misgivings to myself and didn't object when he was given such an important task when he left school. My task was just as important—to mold and shape young minds here is a privilege."

Emmy cringed. It sounded more like brainwashing kids. Why was he telling her all this? He was giving her a lot of information, information she could take to the police. He must not be planning on letting her out of here. She swallowed down the panic that clutched at her throat. He was telling her things about her dad, but it wasn't out of the goodness of his heart. He must be trying to coax her into revealing something he wanted to know, and then he wouldn't need her anymore.

Jonas grabbed at the back of his neck and rubbed it like he was trying to blot out a bad memory. "Pathetic. All his self-righteousness… He just didn't have the stomach to do what needed to be done. He pretended he was on our side, and then he crippled us."

Pride flickered in Emmy's chest. Her dad had *done* something, something to stop them. "What did he do?"

Jonas stopped pacing and looked straight into Emmy's eyes. "He stole something."

Emmy licked her lips. The medallion in her pocket seemed to double in weight.

She could lie and say she didn't know what he was talking about…or she could just hand the medallions over and be done with it. Maybe then he would let her go. Then again, he might not. If Jonas really wanted those medallions, they might be her best bargaining chip. If she could figure out why they were so important, maybe she could use it to her advantage.

"Why do you need that medallion?" Emmy said carefully. "Obviously you can get down here just fine without it. There must be hundreds of medallions like the one somebody sent me."

"You know perfectly well that there was more than one medallion in that box," said Jonas.

So, the medallion she used to get down here wasn't the one he was looking for. That meant each medallion did something different. And Jonas must not have the complete set. "Are you missing one?"

"There was only one complete collection," Jonas said. "It is passed from one Brother Loyola down to the next. Without it, we can't access all the resources we have worked so hard to collect and preserve."

Resources. That meant money. "Are you running out of cash? I thought you'd be rolling in it with all the illegal stuff you do. Can't you just knock over a bank?"

Jonas's mouth twitched. "We always have money coming in, but we use it just as quickly. Every time we expand our reach, we need new funds. When your father took the medallions, it meant we couldn't get what we needed."

Emmy was starting to see things more clearly. When her dad took the medallions, it was like he took their house keys. Only these keys were a lot more valuable. "There are rooms you can't open. Rooms with money—like vaults."

"Rooms with resources," he corrected, "but yes, they are vaults. The monks at Blacehol Abbey built them to preserve their collection of art and antiquities. The last abbot of Blacehol passed that collection to the first Brother Loyola. When Catholics were being persecuted, the vaults were the perfect place for them to hide their valuables. Some of those valuables went unclaimed, and in times of great need, the Order has sold some of those objects to keep afloat.

"This is one of those times. We need to access our vaults, so we can continue to move forward." Jonas started walking toward her. "You have something of mine."

Emmy took a step back. "I don't have anything of yours."

"You're not a very good actress. There's only one way you could have gotten down here tonight."

The sound of his footsteps ricocheted off the ceiling. One step. Two steps. *Closer. Closer.* Emmy needed to get out of here, but how? The only corridor she could navigate was blocked, and who knew where the other ones would take her? The Lane was a maze that she could get lost in for days, but Jonas probably knew it like the back of his hand. If Emmy was going to make a break for it, she needed a way to even the odds.

She glanced at the lanterns that hung between the archways. Maybe, just *maybe*, they could give her what she needed. "If I *did* have that box, and I gave it to you… Would you let me go?"

"Of course." His answer came quick as lightening. Emmy swallowed. He was lying.

"You're right," Emmy said. "Somebody did send me a box. But it wasn't complete—most of the spaces were empty." She looked straight into Jonas's eyes with her most blank expression. *Please let this be a convincing lie.* "I can give you what I have, though."

Jonas closed his eyes and smiled. He believed her.

She pulled her bag off her shoulder and held it up to a lantern, so she could see inside it.

"You won't regret this, young miss."

She put her fingers on the bag's zipper and took a deep breath. Then she grabbed a lantern off its hook and flung it at Jonas with all her might. The flame blew out, but the sound of shattering lantern glass and garbled yelling told her she'd hit her mark. She swung the bag over her shoulder and ran as fast as she could, zigzagging from corridor to corridor like she was running a soccer drill.

Jonas's footsteps started echoing off the walls, and Emmy couldn't tell where they were coming from. Her only hope was that her footsteps would be just as confusing.

She ran through countless archways and rooms. *An exit. There has to be an exit.* Finally, a set of long slippery steps appeared. They were so steep she used her hands for balance and clambered up them like a ladder. Footsteps banged on the stairs below. They were a long way down, but they were approaching fast. She could see a crack of light ahead. *Just a little farther.*

She reached the top. It was a trapdoor. She flung it open and hoisted herself through. She only had a few seconds before Jonas would catch up to her.

The cold air took her breath away. Wind whistled through stone that loomed around her like a fortress. Where was she? She looked around the little round room. There was no door.

An iron staircase wound its way upward, and Emmy jumped on it. The iron clattered and banged, telling Jonas exactly where she was, but she had no choice but to keep going up. The stairs climbed through the ceiling and onto a wrought-iron floor. Giant windows without glass let in blasts of icy wind. A huge bell hung down over a gaping hole that looked onto the room below. She looked around and her shoulders sagged. There was no door here, either. Jonas's footsteps clanged on the iron stairs. She was trapped.

Jonas walked slowly up the last few steps, his face bloodied and burned. Emmy lifted her chin. She had aimed the lantern well. Jonas stepped toward her.

"Take one more step, and I'll scream!" she yelled. "We're not underneath the school anymore. Someone will hear me up here!"

Jonas laughed. "Not out here, love. Haven't you figured out where we are?"

She'd never been in here before. There was nothing in this little round room except the massive bell. It hung between them, its thick rope dangling down through the hole and touching the floor of the room below.

Her insides deflated. "We're in the belfry of the round-tower church."

"Very good." Jonas pointed to the closest building. "Even

the teachers' housing is too far away to hear us. I'm sorry it had to come to this, but you've given me no choice. That box is the best hope we have to carve out our future." He took a knife out of his pocket. "Hand it over, or I'll have to take it one way or another. You'd be amazed by what I can pass off as an accident."

Accident. That's what Jack had called it when Brynn left him in the forest all night. That's what Jonas had said about her dad's friend being seriously hurt. That's what everyone called it when Malcolm fell off the chapter house roof. But none of those things were accidents, and neither was this.

Emmy crouched down and fumbled in the dark for the bag's zipper. The moonlight, which shone straight onto Jonas's battered face, didn't reach to the floor.

Jonas held the knife higher and reached with his other hand. "Pass the box slowly."

She pulled it out of her bag. It was strange to think she'd never see it again. She'd spent so long keeping it away from the Order. She wasn't about to give that up now.

Emmy reached back and hurled it out the giant window.

"No!" Jonas screamed. He lunged his arms out the next window, but the box was already swallowed up by darkness. It belonged to the North Sea now.

Jonas smashed his hand against the wall and screamed again. He looked back at Emmy, his mouth twisted into a snarl. "You're going to wish you hadn't done that."

Emmy could barely breathe. There was nobody to rescue her, nobody to ask for help. She was alone. And she was out of ideas. "There will be a lot of questions. Questions about the Order. Someone will figure out it was you."

Blood was dripping down Jonas's face and splotching onto the iron floor. "I'll have plenty of time to sort that out. No one even knows we're up here."

Emmy's heart stopped. That was it. That was the answer. If only she could make it happen. "You're right." Emmy took two steps back. "No one knows we're here."

Suddenly she sprang forward, leapt over the hole, and wrapped her hands around the rope. It tightened. And the bell started to ring.

The sound was deafening. Jonas clamped his hands over his ears and looked straight at the teachers' housing. Lights were starting to turn on.

He growled and lunged for her. She slackened her grip and slid down into the next room, her bag banging against her back. He couldn't reach her here. There was shouting outside the teachers' dorms. Just a few more minutes and she'd be safe.

The rope jolted. Jonas was furiously sawing through it. If she stayed where she was, the rope would break, and she'd crash twenty feet down onto the stone floor. If she slid down to the ground, where could she go? She twisted her body and looked all around. There had to be a way out.

Finally, she saw a crack of light, a dim outline that didn't fit with the stones around it. It reached all the way down to the floor. The outline of a door.

The rope jolted again. Jonas had almost cut through it. She slid down the rope, jumping the last few feet and hurling herself at the crack. The stones swung open and she flew into a new room. She heard Jonas thundering down the iron steps and she ran into the darkness, as far from his footsteps as possible. A light flashed into her eyes. Arms wrapped around her, and she screamed.

CHAPTER 22

The Other Side of the Door

"Emmy—"

"Get your hands off me!"

"Emmy, it's all right. What's going on?"

The blinding light flickered off and a new light flooded the room. Emmy was in the chapel of the round-tower church, and it wasn't Jonas holding her. It was Barlowe. Madam Boyd stood in the entryway with her hand on an old light switch. Jack and Lola were standing behind her.

Emmy pointed at the door that led to the tower. "It's Jonas. He attacked me."

Barlowe let go of her and tore into the belfry.

Madam Boyd walked toward her, the sound of her cane echoing off the floor. "Emmy, what are you talking about?" Her lips had gone white.

Emmy looked at Jack and Lola. "It wasn't Larraby, it was Jonas the whole time."

Lola swore, and her mother didn't bother to admonish her.

"When you didn't meet us back at the square, we went to get help," Lola said. "Mum got Barlowe, and when we told him the direction you took, he figured out where you'd come out of the tunnels."

"Emmy, what were you saying about Jonas?" Madam Boyd's voice cracked.

"He attacked me," Emmy said, "at the top of the tower. I rang the bell and found the hidden door, and he—" Emmy stopped. Why hadn't Jonas come through the door yet? He was right behind her.

Barlowe came back through the tower door. "There's nobody in the belfry."

No. That couldn't be right. He couldn't have escaped. "He must have gone back into the tunnels." She ran back into the belfry and searched the stone floor. Where was the trapdoor? "It was right here, the entrance to the tunnels was right here!" But there was no handle, no latch, and all the stones looked the same. There was no light in the tunnels to show an outline. Emmy stumbled back into the church. Jonas was gone. She grabbed the back of one of the benches. The church was starting to spin.

Madam Boyd grabbed her arm. "I think you'd better sit down."

Emmy pulled her backpack off her shoulders and sank onto the bench. There was no way to prove what had happened. Nothing to back up her story. She sat with her head in her hands until more teachers started pouring into the church.

"Who the devil broke into the tower?"

"What's all this racket?"

"Why is someone ringing the tower bell at four o'clock in the bloody morning?"

Emmy wrapped her arms around her middle and started to shake. There were so many people, so many questions.

Madam Boyd put a gentle hand on Emmy's shoulder and looked at her with anxious eyes. "I think Master Barlowe and I can deal with this on our own."

The other teachers filed out, muttering to each other about pranks and late-night hijinks.

"All right, why don't you start at the beginning," Madam Boyd said.

It took a long time for Emmy to get through the story. The only thing she left out was the medallions. Jonas would have killed her to get them, and she wasn't about to tell anyone else that they existed. She was vague about how they got down into the tunnels, but nobody asked her for more details. They didn't interrupt her or ask any questions, though Madam Boyd pressed her lips tight together when Emmy talked about Jonas's knife. When Emmy finally stopped talking, nobody said a word.

She closed her eyes. Her hands burned from the rope, and her shoulders ached from carrying her bag all night. She just wanted this to be over.

"That's quite a story," Master Barlowe finally said. "Filled with very serious accusations."

Emmy's lip wobbled. They didn't believe her. They probably all thought she was a liar, just trying to get out of being caught pulling a prank.

Master Barlowe's face was like stone. He kept staring at Emmy, like he was trying to read her mind. "We all know that there are students who will say anything to get out of trouble."

A knot clenched inside Emmy's gut. She was going to be punished. Maybe even expelled.

"But we also know that you are not one of those students."

Hot tears stung Emmy's eyes. They believed her. It was going to be okay.

Madam Boyd stood up and leaned on her cane. "We should be able to pass this all off as a prank that went wrong."

"What do you mean?" Lola asked. "Aren't we going to expose the Order?"

"Not this time. They're just too strong. The Order has a lot of connections. Besides, the board won't allow the school's reputation to get dragged through the mud."

"But they can't just let Jonas keep working here after all he's done," Lola said.

"I doubt we'll find him now," Barlowe said. "The Lane stretches on for miles, and Jonas knows if he stuck around he'd be facing serious charges. I'm sure he's long gone."

The knot in Emmy's stomach loosened a little. Jonas was gone. And it didn't sound like he was coming back. Then she frowned. Barlowe called the tunnels "the Lane." She'd only heard Order members call it that.

"What about Larraby?" Jack asked. "He might not be Brother Loyola, but he's part of the Order, too."

Madam Boyd smiled grimly. "Jameson Larraby has been teaching at this school for years, and he's extremely friendly with the board. It's Emmy's word against his, and I think we all know whose word those old snobs would take seriously."

Lola threw herself back on the bench and huffed, but she didn't protest. Boyd was right. They all knew no one would believe Emmy.

"I think Emmy should be checked out at the medical center," Madam Boyd said. "Then we'll call her mother and—"

"No!" Emmy jumped to her feet. "You can't tell my mom!"

"Emmy, I am responsible for what happens to you at school," Madam Boyd said. "It would be inexcusable for me not to tell her when you have been in such danger."

"But she'll blab!" Emmy wasn't just worried about her mom freaking out. She was worried about what her mom might say to the countless reporters who would take her phone call in a heartbeat. "My mom will never stay quiet about the Order. They'll come after her."

Madam Boyd pursed her lips. "I'll consider it. In the meantime, you need to get to the medical center."

"I'll take her," Barlowe said quickly.

"Good. I'll take the others back to the house."

Madam Boyd ushered Jack and Lola to the door.

Emmy stood up and threw her backpack over her aching

shoulders. She just wanted to get some sleep. She walked toward the door, but Master Barlowe wasn't following her.

"Aren't we going to the medical center?"

"In a minute. We should probably finish our conversation first."

Emmy shivered. There was no heat in the church, and the wind sliced through every crack in the stone walls. "Did you want to ask me something else?"

Barlowe stood up. "You had a medallion, right? That's how you got down onto the Lane?"

Emmy didn't say anything. He had called it "the Lane" again.

"My guess is you have an entire box filled with them."

Something started pulsing in Emmy's neck. "How did you know that?"

"I'll explain everything, but first I'd like you to tell me what happened to that box."

"I threw it out the window," Emmy said, "into the sea."

Barlowe gripped a church pew and closed his eyes.

"Their destruction is not what I would have wanted."

Why wouldn't he want the medallions destroyed? Unless… but he couldn't be. Images started flashing in Emmy's mind. Barlowe trying to get her to leave Latin Society. Barlowe annoyed when she had found a book about the school's founding. Barlowe looking flustered when she said her father's name. *Barlowe. Barlowe.*

"You're part of the Order." She dashed toward the door, but Barlowe stepped in front of her.

"Emmy, please, let me explain."

"HELP!" She tried to shove her way past him, but he was too strong. "Madam Boyd, come back! Barlowe's part of the Order!"

"Calm down, Emmy, I'm not part of the Order! I've spent all year trying to keep you away from them."

"What are you talking about?"

"I tried to get you away from Latin Society and tried to keep you from telling anyone about Tom. But it was already too late."

Emmy stopped pushing. "Tom. You knew my dad?"

Barlowe nodded. "I still know him. I was the one who told him you were coming to Wellsworth. I saw your name on a late enrollment list. I've been helping him communicate with you all year."

"But...but that must mean you know where he is!"

"I wish I did." Barlowe sank into a bench. "We figured out a secure method of communication a long time ago, one that doesn't require me to know his whereabouts. It's safer for all of us."

The pounding in Emmy's chest slowed down and was replaced by a dull ache. "Does anyone else know where he is?"

Barlowe fiddled with the collar on his pajama shirt. "Thomas Allyn is a complicated man with a complicated history. He and I shared a flat with Madam Boyd and another girl. We all became very close. Margaret needed extra help at first because her knee had been badly damaged in…well, an 'incident' in our last year at school."

An incident. Like an accident. "Madam Boyd was the girl who was injured in the initiation ritual. The one that went wrong."

Barlowe tipped his head. "I didn't know you knew about that. You probably know a lot of things that would surprise me."

Emmy looked at the floor. She'd learned a lot about the Order, but she still didn't know where her dad was.

"We started working against the Order, trying to undermine them. Tom was the most brazen. He was still technically a member of the Order, and when an opportunity came up to cripple them, he took it. The Order was coming after him, so he faked his death in a car crash. I was the only one who knew he was still alive. As far as I know, I'm still the only one who knows. Aside from you, now."

"What about Madam Boyd?" Emmy asked.

Barlowe shook his head. "She always thought the Order killed Tom, although she doesn't know what to believe now. She was completely shocked when she found out he was your father. I pretended I didn't know anything about it. The more I tell her, the more likely it is that the Order might go after her."

"She made me swear not to tell anyone about my dad."

Barlowe nodded. "She was desperate to make sure no one else ever found out about your connection with Tom. She knew you'd be in danger, and she didn't want you drawn into this mess." He cleared his throat.

"I can only imagine how difficult it's been for you. Wondering what had happened to him, wondering if he had just left…" His voice trailed off.

Emmy tucked her hair behind her ear. Barlowe had once said he had a complicated relationship with his father, too. Maybe he understood her situation pretty well. But she still wasn't ready to talk about it. At least not with the person who had helped her father stay hidden all these years.

"I can tell you this, Emmy. Tom never would have left you unless it was absolutely necessary for your protection. He loves you."

"Has he ever actually said that he loves me?"

Barlowe looked at his hands. "We don't generally discuss things of a personal nature."

"Then maybe you don't know him as well as you think."

Barlowe didn't say anything. He just kept folding up his pajama collar and then fixing it again.

"Why didn't you want the medallions destroyed?" Emmy asked. "Isn't it a good thing if the Order can never get them?"

"If Tom had wanted them destroyed he would have done it ages ago. He wanted them to stay hidden until we could figure out how best to use them." Barlowe sighed. "But it's probably for the best. Now that they're gone, there's no reason for the Order to come after you."

Emmy shifted in her chair and rubbed the back of her neck. Every inch of her ached.

"We should get you to the medical center, so you can see a nurse."

Emmy nodded. It had been the longest night of her life.

The sun was coming up over the cliffs now, sending a little bit of warmth through Emmy's bare arms. She and Barlowe walked along the path that led back down to the school.

"There's one thing I don't understand," Emmy said. "If you wanted to keep me away from the Order, why did you have me wash walls where that secret entrance is?"

Barlowe smiled. "I never dreamed you'd find the entrance, especially because I specifically told you not to wash that wall. I'm not used to students taking on extra punishment. I guess I underestimated your drive to be the best at everything, even detention."

Barlowe stopped walking and looked at Emmy. "That drive seems to have served you well tonight. I'm sure your father will be very proud."

Emmy shut her eyes up tight. She wasn't sure about anything when it came to her father. But she didn't want to cry again. She turned back toward the school, and they walked in silence the rest of the way.

CHAPTER 23

Saying Goodbye

It took half an hour for the nurse practitioner to finish examining Emmy. "You'll be fine," she said. "Just take it easy for a few days. I'll make sure you get time to rest before finishing up your exams. You'd better spend the day in here, so I can keep an eye on you."

Emmy nodded and lay down on the bed. She was just about asleep when she heard the door click and ease open.

"Hey, Emmy," somebody whispered, "you still awake?"

Emmy opened her eyes and smiled. She was wondering how long it would take Jack and Lola to sneak in here.

"So?" Lola said. "Tell us everything you left out when the adults were listening."

"It's pretty much the same," Emmy said, "other than the box, obviously."

"You didn't tell anyone the truth?" Jack asked.

"No way," Emmy said. "Jonas would have killed me to get that box, and I bet he's not the only one. I'm not telling anyone." Emmy pulled two medallions out of her pocket. "Do you still have the ones I gave you?"

Both Jack and Lola nodded. "Good thing you thought of giving them to us in case we ran into anyone from the Order," Jack said.

"At least the medallions are still safe," Emmy said.

"And you're safe, too," Lola said. "Jonas thinks the medallions are gone, so there's no point in coming after you."

"It's too bad about that pewter box, though," Jack said. "It was so beautiful."

Emmy smiled. "You don't think I brought the real box down there with me, do you?"

Jack raised his eyebrows.

"It was the decoy box?" Lola asked. "The one you put the medallions in after the break-in?"

Emmy nodded. "I'm pretty sure it was too dark for Jonas to see the difference."

"What are you going to do with the medallions now?" Jack asked.

"I don't know," Emmy said. "Put them back in their real box, take them home, and figure out what to do next, I guess."

There was a knock on the door and the nurse practitioner came in. "Ahem, the patient is supposed to be resting. And I believe you two have exams to be studying for."

Jack and Lola quickly left the room, and Emmy closed her eyes again. She should really be studying, but before she could give it a second thought, she was fast asleep.

Emmy didn't wake up until the evening. Madam Boyd told her she'd be given a few extra days to rest before taking her last exams. By the time they were done, it was the last day of school, and her mom was on her way to pick her up.

Emmy hadn't told her mom about what happened in the tower—not exactly. She said someone had dared her to ring the bell and she'd lost her grip and almost fallen. Madam Boyd must not have told her what really happened, at least not yet, because her mom gave her a huge lecture on not blindly doing dares that were dangerous.

When her last exam was done, Emmy met Jack and Lola in the common room.

"How was it?" Lola asked.

"I'm just glad it's over."

"Are you talking about the exam or about the school year?" Jack asked.

"Both, I guess."

Jack bit his lip. "You're *sure* you want to come back?"

Emmy didn't answer right away. She'd been giving this a lot of thought, but she hadn't really said it out loud yet. "I'm no safer at home than I am here. At least there are people here to look out for me, and I think Barlowe's right. Now that Jonas has been uncovered as the head of the Order, he'll probably lay low for a while."

"But don't you feel...I don't know...weird?" Jack asked. "About coming back to the place where someone tried to kill you?"

Emmy shuffled her feet. She still had trouble falling asleep, and she shuddered every time she saw the round-tower church. But when she thought of returning to Connecticut, she felt a pang in her chest that wouldn't go away. "It doesn't matter if it feels weird. This is my home. I'm not going to let a bunch of thugs drive me away."

Lola put her arm around her shoulder, and Emmy winced. Her whole body still ached.

"You'll be fine," Lola said. "Come on, let's get your stuff."

When Emmy and Lola got upstairs, they found Victoria lounging on the bed with a magazine while her mother's maid packed her things. Emmy pressed her lips together. She'd really hoped Victoria would be gone by now.

Lola started tossing things into Emmy's suitcase. She threw a stack of class notes in the garbage, and Emmy quickly fished them out. Victoria's maid zipped up her last bag and started heaving it toward the stairs. It looked like it was at least twice her body weight.

Lola dumped the last of Emmy's clothes into her suitcase and sat down on top of it.

"You know, I think if you fold them—"

"Nope, it's good!" Lola yanked the bulging zipper shut and dragged the bag into the hallway.

Thunk. Thunk. Thunk.

Emmy laughed. She hoped that suitcase was strong enough to survive a trip down three flights of stairs with Lola.

It was just Victoria in the room now. Emmy looked away. What was she supposed to say to a roommate who hated her? Victoria looked up and stopped flipping through her magazine.

She must have realized they were alone. She put the magazine in her purse, pulled out a compact, and studied her reflection. She snuck a few glances at Emmy in the mirror. "I didn't do it, you know."

Emmy wrinkled her forehead. "Didn't do what?"

"I didn't trash all your stuff after the football tournament."

"Oh, yeah. I know." Emmy had almost forgotten she'd even suspected Victoria.

"You lasted a lot longer here than I thought you would," Victoria said. "I figured you'd be back home with your mum within a month."

Emmy crossed her arms. "Why's that?"

"You were getting teary almost every time I came into the room. I couldn't say one word to you without the waterworks starting. I've been a boarder since I was seven years old. I've heard girls cry into their pillows all night and beg their mums to come get them. Tears solve nothing. They just make you weaker."

Emmy stared at Victoria. "Your parents sent you to boarding school when you were seven years old?" She couldn't imagine it.

Victoria smoothed out her hair. "I barely even remember living with my parents."

"Don't you spend the summer with them?"

"They're usually traveling. There's always some nanny at home to look after me in the summer, not that I need it anymore."

Some nanny. It sounded like Victoria didn't even know who she'd find when she got home.

"Do you miss them?"

Victoria adjusted the locket around her neck. "They send me stuff, that's good enough for me."

Emmy pictured a seven-year-old Victoria on her first night at boarding school. Little blond pigtails, clutching a teddy bear, telling herself that tears solved nothing. They wouldn't make her parents care.

Victoria's maid came back into the room. "Your things are ready, miss."

Emmy cleared her throat. "I guess this is goodbye."

Victoria snapped the compact shut and stuffed it into her purse. "Let's hope so." She slung her bag over her shoulder and left, her fancy sandals clacking all the way down the stairs.

When Lola came back, she had a reluctant-looking Jack with her.

"Oh, relax. I saw Victoria leave," Lola said. "No one's going to rat you out for being in a girl's room on the last day."

Jack slipped inside and quickly shut the door.

Lola handed Emmy an envelope. "Someone left this in my mailbox."

Emmy's stomach started to churn. Another envelope? She wasn't even sure she wanted to open it. She'd had enough adventure for a while. She took the envelope and pried open the edge. There wasn't much point in putting it off. She knew she'd open it eventually.

There was a small piece of paper inside. She pulled it out and read it aloud:

Forgive John for telling me where you'd be,
though he doesn't know where I am.
Forgive my cryptic notes, they could
have fallen into the wrong hands.
Forgive me for pretending to be a priest,
I was desperate to catch a glimpse of you.
I won't ask you to forgive my absence,
even though it haunts me.

"Pretending to be a priest?" Jack asked. "What's that about?"

"The Christmas concert," Emmy said. "A priest offered to check my coat, and when I got the coat back, the letter was in the pocket." She had seen her dad, spoken to him, and she hadn't even known it.

"And John," Lola said, "that's Master Barlowe, right?"

Emmy nodded. She still didn't know how she felt about Barlowe lying to her all year long. He did genuinely seem to care though, and that counted for something.

Jack leaned against the door. "So, I guess your dad really is alive. That's great."

"Yeah, I guess," Emmy said.

"Isn't that what you've always wanted?"

Emmy shrugged. "He faked his death twice, and I haven't heard from him in ten years. How am I supposed to feel about that?"

"He faked his death to protect you," Jack said. "That's got to count for something."

"I know," Emmy said. "But then why did he send me all those clues that pushed me toward the Order?"

Lola sat on the edge of the bed. "It was only a matter of time before they figured out who you were. Your dad probably sent you all those clues so you'd be prepared to face them."

"Maybe," Emmy mumbled.

"What else could it be?"

Emmy was quiet for a few moments. "I don't know.

Sometimes I think it's more than that. Sometimes I wonder if maybe he wants me to finish whatever he started when he stole that box fifteen years ago."

Jack and Lola both stared into space, not saying anything. Emmy looked at the letter again. *I won't ask you to forgive my absence, even though it haunts me.* Well, that was one thing they had in common. His absence haunted her, too.

The common room was busy that afternoon. Parents were coming in and out, and students were hugging and promising to meet during the holidays. Most students seemed excited to be going home. Emmy was anything but. *This place'll be in your blood.* That's what Jonas had once told her. Well, maybe there was one thing that he'd been right about.

There was one person who seemed even more miserable than Emmy. Jack looked downright depressed.

"Maybe they won't be so bad this summer," Lola said to him as they pulled their luggage to the car park.

Jack grimaced. "Any room for me in your suitcase?"

"Oh, come off it. You'll be fine," Lola said.

A black Jaguar pulled into the drive. "Bloody hell, that's

them," Jack grumbled. The car stopped right in front of the fountain and a driver jumped out. He ran to the sidewalk and grabbed Jack's suitcases.

"Good afternoon, Master John," the driver said.

Emmy blinked. *Master John?*

He pulled Jack's suitcases to the car, where a man with dark sunglasses and tidy hair was getting out of the back seat.

"That's your dad?" Emmy asked.

"Yep," Jack said.

Emmy shuffled her feet. It was strange to see another member of the Order, even if it was Jack's father. Malcolm walked up to his dad and shook his hand. He smiled at Malcolm, then scanned the crowd of students. When he saw Jack, his face fell into a dark frown.

"You know," Lola said, "you probably could have picked a less antagonizing outfit."

Jack was wearing ripped jeans and a T-shirt with some guy named Alice Cooper on the front. He looked like he might be eating a guitar.

Jack smirked. "Yeah, I suppose I could have. You'll write to me this summer, right?"

Lola snorted, but Emmy nodded and gave Jack a hug. He

walked slowly toward the car, shook his dad's hand, and got into the back seat.

"He's going to be okay, right?" Emmy asked.

"Oh, yeah, he'll be fine," Lola said. "He just doesn't like being told what to do. Not like me—I'm always obedient." She winked and zipped up her hoodie. "Gotta run, we're catching a train to Glasgow tonight, and I haven't started packing yet." She took off and disappeared around the corner.

"There you are!" Emmy's mom was running toward her as fast as her stilettos would go.

"Mom!"

Her mom flung her arms around her, clutching her so tight it almost knocked the wind out of her. "Darling, are you all right? I've been so worried."

"I'm fine, Mom, really. It was just a stupid dare."

Her mom crouched down and looked her square in the eye. "Emmy, I talked to Madam Boyd yesterday."

Emmy's heart sank. If her mom knew what had happened in the tower, she could kiss Wellsworth goodbye. "What did she say?"

Her mom smiled. "She told me you were an exemplary student who had risen beyond all her expectations. She said you'd faced many challenges, and that you'd met them head-on. She's very proud of you."

"She said that?" A warm rush flooded Emmy's cheeks.

"She did. Listening to her talk about how well you're doing made me miss you even more." She tucked a strand of Emmy's hair behind her ear. "I'm proud of you, too, Em. Looks like I'll be sending you to a more challenging school at home next year."

The warm rush vanished. "Home? But Mom, Wellsworth *is* my home."

"Darling, don't be ridiculous. I'm glad you've done so well while I was away but filming this TV show is over now. I can't profess to be a parenting expert if my twelve-year-old daughter lives on a different continent."

Of course, this was about her mother's career. Emmy should have known. That's what it's always about.

"And…" her mom hesitated, "I'd miss you too much. This year without you just… It hasn't been the same."

Emmy looked down at her toes. It was nice to hear her mom say that. There had definitely been times when she'd wished her mom was close by. Maybe going back to Connecticut wouldn't be so bad.

She looked around the parking lot and saw the main

building rising above her. Its towers and spires had been so intimidating on her first day. It had made her think of an old cathedral that nobody went to anymore. Now it made her think of Saint Audrey's Feast Day, and getting lost in an endless library, and Master Barlowe bringing Shakespeare to life. Mostly it made her think of Jack and Lola, of having lunch in the Hall and laughing about who knows what.

She looked at her mom and bit her lip. "Even though you won't be filming, you'll still be away a lot. And you'll be busy writing and doing research and giving speeches. When I'm at Wellsworth, there's always someone looking out for me."

Her mom shifted her weight. "But what would I tell people?"

"You'll tell them the truth! That I love it here. And," she grinned, "as a child psychologist and as my mother, you know what's best for me. It would be unhealthy to rip me away from such a rich learning environment."

Her mom smirked. "Do I really sound like that?"

"Sometimes." Emmy laughed, and then bit her lip. "Please, Mom, seriously. You can't take me away."

"I don't know…" Her mom tipped her head. "Madam Boyd did sound lovely on the phone."

"She's the best! Her daughter is one of my best friends!"

"Oh, there are families here?"

"Sure!" She didn't mention that the Boyds were the only family on campus. That was another one of those things her mother didn't need to know.

"Well, I should at least look around the school and meet some of the teachers before I decide. Maybe Madam Boyd and her daughter could show us around."

"I'm sure they'd love to." If anyone could convince her mom to let her stay, it would be the Boyds.

"Oh yes, there was one thing Madam Boyd mentioned that surprised me." Her mom narrowed her eyes. "She said what an exceptional asset you were on the soccer team."

Oh. Right. Emmy scratched her ear. "Yeah, uh, about that..."

"I guess it didn't hamper your studies too much, but we're still going to talk about it later."

Emmy breathed a sigh of relief. Her mom didn't sound *too* mad. She led her mom toward Audrey House, looking at the sprawling grounds, breathing in the salty air, and smiling. A vacation in Connecticut would be nice. But in two months, she'd be ready to come back to school. Back home.

Acknowledgments

I am so grateful to the entire team at Sourcebooks. To Annie Berger, thank you for being my champion and for caring so deeply about my story. I also thank Sarah Kasman, Cassie Gutman, and Becca Sage for all your editorial work. To Jordan Kost and Hannah Peck, thank you for creating a cover so stunning that when I first saw it, I literally screamed in my agent's ear.

To Brenda Drake and Heather Cashman, thank you for your tireless work on Pitch Wars, which literally changed my life. Speaking of Pitch Wars, I can't go any further without thanking Julie C. Dao. Julie, thank you for choosing me out of nowhere to be your mentee. Your support and advice forever changed the way I write.

I have the most amazing tribe of writers who help and push

me every day. Thank you to all my beta readers and critique partners, including Tara Creel, Suzi Guina, Alli Jayce, Kit Rosewater, Lacee Little, and Laura Lashley. Your feedback, and your friendship, is woven into the fabric of this novel.

To my agent, Melissa Edwards, thank you for working so tirelessly on my book. Your editorial suggestions transformed the manuscript into a novel, and I am so grateful for how much you put into my writing and my career every day.

To Joel and Tracy, and to Karl and Steph, thank you for making me laugh every time we're in the same room. To Benjamin and Matthew, thank you for never being afraid to show the world your true selves. To my dear Katherine, thank you for being my first real reader, and for giving me feedback that was far more advanced than I could have imagined. To Judy, thank you for reading my first draft, and for being honest while still finding ways to avoid telling me that it sucked. As always, thank you for being not just my cousin, but for being my sister, too.

To my parents, thank you for your never-ending support and encouragement. Dad, thank you for all the time you've spent looking after Audrey so I could write, teach, and feel like a normal person. Mom, I'm so glad you were able to read an early draft of this novel, even though you were already so sick.

Thank you for making sure that I know how proud you would be of me right now, even though you can't tell me.

To my darling Audrey, you are my heart. Always.

Finally, to Jason, thank you for being my plot magician. Thank you for being my rock. Thank you for being my love.

About the Author

Julia Nobel is a teacher on an island off the south coast of Canada. By the time she was ten, she had a beloved notebook filled with plot ideas for novels and TV shows. Even though she hadn't read them in years, she cried when she had to get rid of her Baby-Sitters Club books because they wouldn't fit in the family's moving truck, and she promptly bought them all again in her new city. Now, she carries another plot-filled notebook, although it's also filled with shopping lists and reminders to feed the cat. She is a writing coach and offers workshops for children, youth, and adults. *The Mystery of Black Hollow Lane* is her debut novel.